# "One Of These Days, Someone Is Going To See Past Your Flirtation To The Truth,"

Logan warned, his voice a husky growl.

It wasn't until he captured her fingers that she realized she'd flattened her palm against his rib cage. She tugged to free her hand, but he tightened his grip.

The sexual tension he roused in her went from simmer to roiling boil. "Let me go."

"You started it."

"What's gotten into you today?"

"You know, I think this is the first time I've ever seen you lose your cool. I like it."

How had he turned the tables on her in such a short time? She pressed her thighs together, but this action made the ache worse, not better.

*What you need is a man who will barge right past your defenses and drive you wild.* Thank goodness he'd never find out just how much she liked the sound of that.

"I'm really not interested in what you—"

She never had a chance to finish the thought. Before she guessed his intention, Logan lowered his lips to hers and cut off her denial.

\* \* \*

**At Odds with the Heiress**
is part of the Las Vegas Nights trilogy:
Where love is the biggest gamble of all!

\* \* \*

If you're on Twitter,
tell us what you think of Harlequin Desire!
#harlequindesire

Dear Reader,

When I decided to set a series of books in Las Vegas, I thought it would be fun to have them be about three half sisters who'd grown up very differently. The first book introduces former child actress Scarlett Fontaine, and security specialist/entrepreneur Logan Wolfe. Against the backdrop of luxury hotels and casinos, these two grapple with their differences as they learn that trusting one another is the best way to happiness.

For those of you familiar with Las Vegas, you may notice that I borrowed heavily (stole outright) from certain casinos on the strip when I created the hotels run by the three Fontaine sisters. I make no apologies. The developers have vision beyond anything I could create and I wanted the best for my girls.

I hope you enjoy Scarlett and Logan's story.

All the best,

Cat Schield

# AT ODDS WITH
# THE HEIRESS

—

## CAT SCHIELD

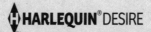
HARLEQUIN® DESIRE

Recycling programs
for this product may
not exist in your area.

ISBN-13: 978-0-373-73292-0

AT ODDS WITH THE HEIRESS

Copyright © 2014 by Catherine Schield

Printed in U.S.A.

www.Harlequin.com

**Books by Cat Schield**

**Harlequin Desire**

*Meddling with a Millionaire* #2094
*A Win-Win Proposition* #2116
*Unfinished Business* #2153
*The Rogue's Fortune* #2192
*A Tricky Proposition* #2214
*The Nanny Trap* #2253
*\*At Odds with the Heiress* #2279

*Las Vegas Nights

Other titles by this author available in ebook format.

---

# CAT SCHIELD

has been reading and writing romance since high school. Although she graduated from college with a B.A. in business, her idea of a perfect career was writing books for Harlequin. And now, after winning the Romance Writers of America 2010 Golden Heart Award for series contemporary romance, that dream has come true. Cat lives in Minnesota with her daughter, Emily, and their Burmese cat. When she's not writing sexy, romantic stories for Harlequin Desire, she can be found sailing with friends on the St. Croix River or in more exotic locales like the Caribbean and Europe. She loves to hear from readers. Find her at www.catschield.com. Follow her on Twitter, @catschield.

To Diane, Rose and Kevin. Thanks for all your support through the years. Researching Vegas wouldn't have been as fun without you!

# One

Logan Wolfe slowed his stride as he entered the fifth floor executive office, taking a moment to appreciate the feminine tableau silhouetted against the backdrop of the Las Vegas Strip. Although all three Fontaine sisters were brunettes of a similar height and bone structure, they could not have been less alike in attitude, style and background.

The three were half sisters who'd known nothing of each other until their common father, Ross Fontaine, died five years ago. When their grandfather, Henry Fontaine, chairman and CEO of the multibillion-dollar Fontaine Hotels and Resorts, found out that Ross had two illegitimate daughters, he tracked them down and brought them into the family fold. They'd both changed their last names to Fontaine and accepted important roles in the company in order to participate in a contest, devised by their grandfather, to see which of his three heirs would run the Fontaine empire when he retired.

"Good morning, Logan," Violet Fontaine called, waving him over. "Grandpa, Logan has joined us."

"Good morning, Logan." Henry Fontaine's deep voice sounded from the speakerphone. He was based in New York City where the company had their corporate office and kept in touch with his granddaughters through a weekly conference call.

"Good morning, Mr. Fontaine. I hope I'm not intruding."

"Not at all," the CEO said. "In fact, I have to run to another meeting. Violet, dear, once again, I'm sorry for your loss. Call me if there's anything I can do for you."

"Thank you, Grandfather."

As Harper Fontaine pushed the button that ended the call, Violet gestured to the empty chair beside her. Logan sat down and gave Violet's hand a sympathetic squeeze.

"I was sorry to hear about Tiberius. How are you holding up?"

Her eyes brimmed with unshed tears. "Even though we all knew he had heart problems, it was still such a shock. He was a live wire. His energy never seemed to stop. I figured he'd live forever."

Logan had been friends with Violet for seven years, since he and his twin brother, Lucas, had decided to expand their growing security company to Las Vegas. Violet was the grounded middle sister who had a girl-next-door charm. Her mother, Suzanne, had been a showgirl at one time, but after a brief affair with Ross Fontaine and the birth of her daughter, she'd gone to work for Tiberius Stone, owner of the Lucky Heart Hotel and Casino. Twenty years her senior, Tiberius had fallen in love with Suzanne and they'd moved in together. Growing up, Violet had shadowed Tiberius around his hotel and by the time she graduated high school she knew more about running a casino than people twice her age.

In fact, Tiberius Stone was the reason the three sisters were solemn this morning. Violet's surrogate father had been found dead of an apparent heart attack in his office at the Lucky Heart the day before.

As Violet dabbed at her eyes, Harper spoke up. "Have you had breakfast, Logan?"

The Fontaine sisters met every Wednesday morning for breakfast at one of the three luxury hotels they managed for their grandfather. Sitting side by side on the Las Vegas Strip, each property was a unique reflection of the sister who ran it. This morning, they were enjoying breakfast at Fontaine Ciel, Harper's property and the newest jewel in the Fontaine crown. Taking a cue from the French word for sky, Harper had designed her sixty-story tower to showcase panoramic views of the Strip. In the most expensive suites, high above the city, eighteen-foot walls of windows were designed to give guests a sense that they were floating just below a dome of intense blue. The signature color was echoed everywhere in the two-billion-dollar hotel.

"Thanks. I've already eaten." He'd been up for three hours already. First his morning workout. A touch-base meeting with Lucas and then the trip to Fontaine Ciel to check the progress of the team testing the security system his company had installed in the soon-to-open hotel. "But I'll take a cup of green tea if Violet doesn't mind sharing."

"There's more than enough for two." Violet's hazel eyes were warm as she filled an empty cup and nudged it over to him. "It's good to see that someone besides me appreciates the virtues of green tea." She looked pointedly at the sister to her left.

"Right," Scarlett murmured, speaking up for the first time. "Heaven forbid Logan would try anything that's bad for him."

Scarlett Fontaine, voluptuous, charismatic and just plain

sexy, had a knack for getting under Logan's skin. In his opinion, the breathtakingly beautiful former actress was the last person who should be running a billion-dollar hotel and casino. Without a college degree or business experience, she relied on her abundant charm to get things done, and it rubbed Logan the wrong way how much she'd accomplished with such techniques.

She popped a bite of sugary pastry into her mouth. Her soft murmur of enjoyment made the hair on Logan's arms stand up. He was a millisecond too slow to brace against the shock wave of awareness. Compelling and unwelcome, lust rushed through him, leaving a destructive tangle of longing and fury in its wake.

From the moment he'd entered the room, he'd done his best to ignore the once-popular child star. Being near her aggravated his composure. She exuded sexual energy the way Harper projected professionalism and Violet radiated optimism. Many times Logan had watched Scarlett shake up a roomful of men by simply appearing in a doorway. That he was similarly affected despite his best efforts to remain immune pissed him off.

He liked things that he could control. Computer systems. Fast cars. Any risks he took were carefully calculated to result in the best possible outcome. "Chance favors the prepared mind" was a motto he lived by. Scarlett would counter with "Fortune favors the bold."

"I've tried plenty of things that are bad for me," he retorted. Avoiding the allure of her witchy green eyes didn't make him immune to their impact. "I like living a healthy lifestyle. Both physically and mentally."

Scarlett gestured with her chin in Violet's direction. "You two are perfect for each other."

Logan agreed. He wanted a woman who matched him. Someone who shared his views about healthy living and maintaining a balance between work and home. Not a fiery siren who would turn his routines upside down and rock his world.

Violet shook her head, the melancholy in her eyes clearing for the moment. "We're too much alike. We'd bore each other to death. No. I think Logan needs someone who will challenge him." Violet got to her feet and aimed a wicked grin at Scarlett. "Someone like you."

There was a slight hesitation before Scarlett's dismissive laugh. Logan cursed his curiosity as he watched the exchange. What had caused the delayed reaction? His pulse spiked. He sat back with crossed arms and watched Violet exit the room. The pause didn't mean Scarlett had considered the idea. She'd never given him any reason to believe she suffered the same sexual attraction that plagued him. Quite the reverse.

In fact, Logan wasn't sure she was interested in any of the men who pursued her. She doled out flirtation like candy that her admirers gobbled up, all the while keeping them at arm's length. Which made them all the more determined to have her.

For the past five years, since she'd left her acting career behind in Los Angeles and moved to Las Vegas to run Fontaine Richesse, Logan had watched her disappoint one suitor after another. He'd decided she was a coldhearted woman who enjoyed tormenting men, and kept his own desires firmly in check. A challenge when she took great pleasure in teasing him.

Shifting his focus to what had brought him to Harper's office this morning, he gave her an accounting of what he'd found during his consultation with his team regarding her security system.

"There won't be any problem having the cameras adjusted before your soft opening," he concluded.

"Good." She'd been making notes as he spoke. "One less thing to worry about." She glanced at her watch. "If there's nothing else, I have a meeting in ten minutes." A line appeared between her brows as she muttered, "That's providing he bothers to show up this time."

"Actually, I did have one more thing," Logan said. "A favor, actually."

He caught Scarlett's sudden interest in his peripheral vision. She leaned her elbows on the table and watched intently. He would have preferred to make his request to Harper in private, but with her hotel opening only ten days away, her time was limited.

"My niece is in town for the rest of the summer and I wondered if she could shadow you for a couple weeks. Observe a businesswoman in action."

Harper, the oldest of the three women by a year, was Ross Fontaine's only legitimate child. She had the training and the ambition to take over for her grandfather when he stepped down in two years. Harper's mother came from old East Coast money and had insisted her daughter be raised in New York City and educated at an Ivy League school. Her style was elegant and professional, from her smooth chignon to her black designer pumps.

"You're the perfect role model," he finished.

"The perfect role model," Scarlett echoed, her throaty voice rich with laughter. "The ultimate professional."

Logan glared at her, realizing he'd laid it on a bit thick. But the task his sister and brother-in-law had handed him was outside of Logan's expertise.

"I'd love to help," Harper retorted. "As soon as the hotel opens."

"I was hoping you could start showing her the ropes sooner."

"I don't know how I can...." Harper sent a hopeful look in Scarlett's direction. "What about you?"

"My schedule is wide-open," Scarlett said, her gaze as steady and watchful as a psychiatrist's. "I'd be happy to help."

This was not at all what Logan had in mind. His relationship with Harper was professional and cordial. What happened between him and Scarlett could only be called acrimonious. His niece was already a troublesome seventeen-year-old. Under Scarlett's influence, the girl would become completely unmanageable.

"Unless Logan doesn't think I'm role-model material," Scarlett continued when he didn't immediately jump on her offer. Her ability to read his mind with unnerving accuracy gave her an unwelcome advantage over him.

"Don't be ridiculous." Harper appeared oblivious to her sister's subtext. "Besides, your hotel is operational. She'll get a much better sense of how things run. Now, if you two will excuse me, I have an internationally famous pain in the ass to meet with."

Logan stared after Harper, cursing his bad timing. He should never have brought up his problem within earshot of Scarlett.

"Tell me about your niece," Scarlett prompted.

"I don't need your help." Being subtle was not the way to handle Scarlett.

"No," she said in a sugarcoated tone, "you don't *want* my help." She added coffee to her cup, lifted the rim to her mouth and blew across the surface. "There's a difference."

Captivated by the small O formed by her bright red lips, he took far too long to respond to her gibe. "Very well," he agreed. "I don't want your help."

"How old is she?"

Logan took a couple seconds to grind his teeth. Despite

being trapped between frustration with his niece and the woman sitting across the table from him, he told her what she wanted to know. "Madison is seventeen. She's my sister's youngest." And in the past three months had driven Paula and her husband, Randolph, past the edge of patience.

"Madison? As in the capital of Wisconsin?"

"As in Madison Avenue." Logan winced. "Her father owns a large ad agency in New York City."

And Paula was a partner in a prestigious law firm. Madison had inherited both brains and ambition from her parents. She'd graduated second in her class and had been accepted to four prestigious universities. If she'd wanted, she could've swiftly climbed any corporate ladder she chose. Instead, to both her parents' horror, the teenager had decided to become an actress.

"And he's hoping she'll follow in his footsteps? From your sour expression I'm guessing that's not what she wants to do."

"She's refusing to go to college. She turns eighteen in two weeks and is determined to move to L.A."

Scarlett's curiosity sharpened. "What's wrong with L.A.?"

"It's not the city, it's her chosen career path."

"Instead of me dragging it out of you one question at a time, why don't you just tell me what's really going on. And why you wanted her to shadow Harper."

Sharing family troubles with outsiders went against the grain, but he desperately needed help. Anyone's help. Even Scarlett's.

"Madison ran away to Los Angeles over spring break. She's determined to become an actress."

Scarlett's full lips twitched. Over the years he'd noticed how well she could read people. Normally he concealed how easily she riled his temper and his hormones, but in this case his sarcastic tone had given too much away.

"The scandal that must have caused your family," she deadpanned.

"She's only seventeen."

"And she could've fallen into someone's evil clutches."

Logan didn't appreciate that she was having fun at his expense. "Thankfully that didn't happen."

"What did happen?"

Not a damn thing. Madison had moved in with a boy she'd met in New York City the summer before and signed up to take an acting class. She'd even gotten a callback for a commercial.

"Her father found her before she got into trouble and brought her back to New York."

"Why don't they just let her follow her dream?" Scarlett poured herself a little more coffee. "Being an actress isn't the worst job in the world."

"Paula and Ran don't think it's the proper career for a girl as bright and capable of going places as Madison," he explained. "They want her to go to college and get a degree."

Other than a brief narrowing of her eyes, Scarlett's expression remained tranquil. "I didn't go to college and I think I'm doing all right."

So said the former child actress whose exploits had kept the paparazzi awash in scandalous photographs for several years. Scarlett's support of Madison's acting dreams was exactly why he hadn't asked her for help.

"You also had a billionaire grandfather bring you to Las Vegas and hand you a hotel to run."

He didn't realize how insulting that sounded until her seductive charm vanished in a flash of annoyance. For the first time ever, Logan believed he'd been granted a glimpse of the genuine woman beneath the mask. And it heightened his already keen awareness of her desirability. He inhaled slowly and let his breath leak out as he wrestled his libido under control. As his blood continued to pulse hot and slow through his veins, he had to repeat his breathing exercise.

Damnation. Why the hell did she have to be so utterly gorgeous?

She had flawless pale skin, dramatic bone structure and a body built to drive a man insane: large firm breasts, tiny waist, lean long legs. The way she moved invited everyone to stare. And her mouth… Her lush, red lips were crafted for kissing.

"You're right," she drawled, her temper giving the words a sarcastic bite. "It's unrealistic to think I would be running Fontaine Richesse if Grandfather hadn't gotten this crazy idea that his granddaughters should compete for the CEO job. I'd still be in L.A., auditioning for roles, working when I could and waiting for the part that would reenergize my career. But I would still be a success and I would be happy."

"Look, I only meant that you never would have been considered as Fontaine Richesse's general manager if you hadn't been Ross's daughter."

For the first time in five years, she'd let him see how much he'd upset her. But all too quickly, she regained her equilibrium. "And you've made it perfectly clear you don't think I belong here."

"I'm not sure you do."

She looked astonished. "Thank you."

"For what?"

"For being honest for once. You've looked down on me from the moment we met." The directness of her gaze demanded he respond with frankness, but his mother had not raised him to insult women.

"I don't look down on you." That wasn't entirely true.

Despite the hotel's success, he didn't think she was in Violet and Harper's league when it came to running a company the size of Fontaine Hotels and Resorts.

"But you don't approve of me, either," she prompted.

"It isn't that I don't approve."

"What is it, then?" She battered him with a determined stare. "You're friendly with my sisters." She paused a beat. "You must have something against me."

"I have nothing against you."

"You believe both Violet and Harper have what it takes to be become the CEO of Fontaine Hotels." She paused for confirmation, but he gave her nothing but stony silence. "And you don't think I do." Again she'd read his mind. When he still didn't respond, her eyes warmed to soft moss. "They've both worked exceptionally hard to get to where they are. I'm a clueless actress. You feel protective of them." She regarded him with a half smile. "You are a good friend, but you don't have to worry. I don't have any business experience, which means I have no chance of besting either of my well-educated, incredibly capable siblings. Grandfather was merely playing fair when he included me in the contest." Her husky voice raked across his nerve endings. She was putting herself down to prevent him from doing so. "I'm so glad we've cleared that up."

They'd cleared up nothing. He was no more comfortable around her or capable of being friendly with her than he'd been five minutes earlier. But what more could he say? He wasn't about to tell her that she'd bewitched him.

"Getting back to your niece and her determination to avoid college," Scarlett continued, her manner becoming brisk and efficient. "What were you hoping she'd discover by shadowing Harper for a couple weeks?"

"That the business world wasn't as much of a drag as she thinks it will be."

Scarlett had a musical laugh, rich with amusement. "And you chose Harper, the workaholic, for her to shadow? She'll die of boredom before the first day is over. She'd do better with Violet." She paused and tapped a spoon on the pristine white tablecloth. "Of course, with Tiberius's death, this isn't a good time for that."

"I agree."

Which brought them back to her. The reality hung unspoken between them.

"Why don't you show her all the interesting aspects of your security business?"

She'd struck right to the heart of his troubles. "Every time I try to engage Madison, she rolls her eyes and starts texting." He made no attempt to hide his frustration. "I thought maybe someone outside the family would have better luck."

Scarlett scrutinized Logan's grim expression. Figuring she'd probably annoyed him enough for one day, she held back a smart-aleck remark about the situation requiring a feminine touch. "You're probably right to think she'll be in a better frame of mind to listen to a disinterested third party."

A disinterested third party with a master's degree in business like Harper, or ten years of hotel and casino management experience like Violet. Not a former child star who had none of the skills required to run a world-class hotel. Logan had been right about that, but his low opinion of her stung. Not that he was wrong. Or alone in his estimation of her failings. She was sure that the same thought had crossed the minds of a dozen hotel and casino owners in Las Vegas. But she hated his disdain more than all the others put together.

Uncomfortable with the direction her thoughts had taken her, Scarlett glanced around her sister's office. The room was a little over the top for her taste. It was almost as if Harper had been feeling insecure when she'd brought in the expensive furnishings and accessories. Which was ridiculous. If anyone could build and run the most successful Fontaine hotel in Las Vegas and become the next CEO, it was Henry Fontaine's only legitimate granddaughter.

"Of course, if you want someone to tell her how hard it is to make it as an actress in Hollywood, I'm your girl." Scarlett tossed her napkin onto the table. "When did you wish her reprogramming to begin?"

Logan scowled at her. It was one of several unhappy expressions he wore whenever they occupied the same space. "If you're not going to take this seriously, I'll wait until Harper or Violet is free."

"I think you're a little too desperate for that." Drawing upon a fifteen-year acting career, Scarlett slapped on a winning smile and stood. "I may not be your first choice for this project, but I'm what you're going to get."

"Fine."

Logan got to his feet and towered over her. "I'll drop Madison off this afternoon at your office. Say, around one?"

"I'll be waiting." She moved away, eager to escape his overwhelming presence, but hadn't taken more than four steps before his hand caught her wrist.

"Thank you." Logan's fingers were gentle on her skin.

He'd never touched her before. The contact sizzled through her like lightning. Unnerved by the strength of her reaction, she twisted free with more vigor than necessary. "It's too late for you to start being nice to me, Logan."

His deep brown eyes developed a layer of ice. "Fine."

He scanned her from her messy updo to her hot-pink toenails, missing nothing in between. Her heart thumped like a runner's feet against the pavement and tension knotted her shoulders. Every time she got within fifty feet of the guy, she turned into an excited teenager with an enormous crush.

And he seemed completely immune.

At six feet two inches tall, the muscled hunk had a commanding presence. He wore his wavy black hair long enough to graze his collar. Bold eyebrows, a strong nose and a square jaw didn't make him classically handsome, but they combined to produce a face worth staring at. His chiseled lips lingered in her daydreams even though when she was around they were always set in a grim line.

"Can you at least wear something business-y?" he demanded, a muscle jumping in his cheek. "Madison needs to spend time with a professional career woman."

Holding perfectly still beneath his criticism was challenging as a combination of sizzling heat and disquieting tingles attacked her composure. In a flowing ankle-length dress cut low in front, and strappy gold sandals, Scarlett knew she looked more like a guest of her Las Vegas hotel than the manager.

"I don't do business-y." She turned on her four-inch heels and strode out of the office, fleeing from feelings of inadequacy.

With his long legs, Logan had little trouble keeping up. "Surely you have something in your vast wardrobe that looks professional."

"What makes you think I have a vast wardrobe?"

"In five years I've never seen you wear the same thing twice."

Stunned that he'd noticed what she wore, much less remembered, Scarlett spared him the briefest glance. "I'm flattered that you've been paying attention," she remarked, using her most flirtatious manner to hide her decidedly smitten response to his observation.

"Don't be. Part of my job as a security expert is to pay attention to details."

"Well, aren't you a silver-tongued devil," she quipped, stepping into the elevator that would take her to the second floor and the skyways that linked the sisters' three Fontaine hotels.

Logan's sleeve brushed her bare arm as he reached past her to punch the button for the lobby. As the doors closed, he lingered in her space, awakening her senses to the coiled strength lurking in his muscles.

Before she considered the imprudence of her action, she poked her finger into his firm abs. "You sure know what to say to make a girl feel special."

She expected him to back off. He'd always kept his distance before. To her shock, he shifted closer. Such proximity to his straightforward masculinity had a disturbing effect on her equilibrium. She had to fight to keep from leaning against him for support.

"Don't you ever get tired of acting?" he mused, his casual tone not matching the dangerous tension emanating from him.

Gathering a shaky breath, she forced the corners of her mouth upward. "What do you mean, acting?"

"The various women you become to fool men into accepting whatever fantasy you want them to believe."

Was he referring to the facade she used to keep Logan in the dark about the way he stirred her body and soul? He was completely mad if he believed she was going to give up her one defense against him.

"Don't you mean the one I use to manipulate them to my will?" she taunted, her breathless tone coming easily under the influence of Logan's domineering presence.

Scarlett prided herself on being able to read men. Usually it was pretty easy. Most of them enjoyed being powerful and having beautiful women available for their pleasure. Even the ones who appeared as sweet as lambs harbored a little caveman inside them.

Logan didn't fall neatly into the bucket where she lumped the rest of his gender. He seemed genuinely immune to her wiles and that's why she provoked him at every opportunity. She was challenged by his lack of physical attraction to her. And in a twisted way, because she knew he'd never step across the line, his indifference gave her the freedom to let her sensuality run free. It was quite liberating.

"One of these days someone is going to see past your flirtation to the truth," Logan warned, his voice a husky growl.

She arched her eyebrows. "Which is what?"

"That what you need isn't some tame lapdog."

"I don't?"

"No." Espresso eyes watched her with lazy confidence. "What you need is a man who will barge right past your defenses and drive you wild."

"Don't be ridiculous," she retorted, struggling to keep her eyes off his well-shaped lips and her mind from drifting into the daydream of being kissed silly by the imposing Logan Wolfe.

"You can lie to yourself all you want," he said. "But don't bother lying to me."

It wasn't until he captured her fingers that she realized she'd flattened her palm against his rib cage. She tugged to free her hand, but he tightened his grip.

The sexual tension he roused in her went from simmer to roiling boil. "Let me go."

"You started it."

She wasn't completely sure that was true. "What's gotten into you today?"

His lips kicked up at the corners. "You know, I think this is the first time I've ever seen you lose your cool. I like it."

How had he turned the tables on her in such a short time? She pressed her thighs together, but this action made the ache worse, not better.

*What you need is a man who will barge right past your defenses and drive you wild.* Thank goodness he'd never find out just how much she liked the sound of that.

"I'm really not interested in what you—"

She never had a chance to finish the thought. Before she guessed his intention, Logan lowered his lips to hers and cut off her denial. Slow and deliberate, his hot mouth moved across hers. Her startled murmur of surprise became a weak moan of surrender as she opened to his tongue slicking over the seam of her lips.

Canting her head to give him better access to her mouth, she slid her fingers into his hair and held on for dear life as her world shifted its orbit. If his intention had been to drive her wild, he achieved his goal in less than three seconds. Every nerve in her body cried out for his touch as he cupped the side of her neck and let his tongue duel with hers.

Scarlett wanted to cry out as she experienced the delicious pleasure of his broad chest crushing her breasts, but he'd stolen her breath. Then the sound of the doors opening reached them both at the same time. Logan broke the kiss. His chest heaved as he sucked in air. Eyes hard and unreadable, he scrutinized her face, cataloging every crack running through her composure. Scarlett felt as exposed as if she'd stepped into her casino wearing only her underwear.

Breathless, she asked, "Did that feel like acting?"

His hands slid away from her in a slow, torturous caress. He stepped back, used his foot to block the doors from closing and gestured her toward the hallway beyond the elevator.

One dark eyebrow lifted. "Needs more investigating before I can say one way or another."

# Two

While his brain throbbed with questions he couldn't answer, Logan drove his black Escalade down Fontaine Ciel's parking ramp and sped toward Wolfe Security. The taste of Scarlett lingered on his tongue. The bitter bite of strong coffee. The sweetness of the sugar he'd licked off the corner of her mouth from the Danish she'd eaten.

July sunshine ricocheted off car windows and punished his vision. Despite the sunglasses perched on his nose, he squinted. Even though it was only a little after nine in the morning, it was already too damn hot. He tugged at his collar and turned the SUV's air conditioner on full blast. Sweat made his shirt cling to him beneath his suit coat. Okay, maybe not all the heat bombarding him came from the temperature outside. Beneath his skin, his blood raged, fierce and unquenchable.

Kissing Scarlett had been a huge mistake. Colossal. If he'd had it bad for her before she'd pressed that sensational body of hers against him, he was now completely obsessed. But it was never going to go any further.

*Needs more investigating…*

What the hell was wrong with him? Giving her a taste of her own tricks had backfired. Not only had he promised to kiss her again, he'd also revealed that he was interested in pursuing her.

He slammed on his brakes and cursed as an out-of-towner cut him off. His phone buzzed. He cued the Escalade's Bluetooth and answered.

"Got your message about Tiberius," Lucas Wolfe said. The poor connection and background noise made his brother hard to understand. "Sorry to hear the old guy's dead."

"I just left the Fontaine sisters. Violet's pretty shaken up."

"I'm sorry for Violet," Lucas muttered. "Did you get a chance to ask her about Tiberius's files?"

Impatience gusted through Logan. "Geez, Lucas. The guy just died."

"And if those files come to light a lot of people both in Vegas and beyond are at risk of having their lives ruined. She could be in danger."

Logan's twin had spent too many years in army intelligence. Lucas saw enemies around every corner. Well, he'd been right to worry on some occasions, maybe even this one. How much dirt could Tiberius Stone have collected over the course of fifty years? In a town dubbed Sin City? A lot.

Logan cursed. "Do you really think they exist?"

"I think he's the J. Edgar Hoover of Vegas."

"I never found any sign of anything in his computers." When Lucas had first gotten wind of Stone's proclivity for information gathering, Logan had hacked into the man's work and personal computers.

"He's old-school," Lucas said. "I'm pretty sure he kept paper copies of everything."

Logan pondered how much information there could be and imagined a large room lined with file cabinets. Where the hell had the old guy stored his papers? The location would have to be secure and accessible. Logan considered. If the data was digital, Wolfe Security would have been the perfect place to keep the information. They had a number of secure servers that their clients used for their most sensitive documents.

"When are you coming back to the States?" Logan asked.

Lucas was in Dubai meeting with a sheikh who had a museum's worth of treasure and art that he wanted displayed in his various homes around the world. The challenge came from his desire for the security to be unobtrusive as well as unbreakable.

"Not sure yet." Lucas's tone darkened. "This job is a lot more complex than I first thought."

"And the daughter?"

"Distracting."

Laughing, Logan hung up with his brother and dialed Violet. He wasn't surprised when the call rolled to voice mail. He left a message asking her to call him back. After that, he put in a couple hours before heading home to have lunch with his niece and break the news that her vacation was officially over.

He found Madison by the pool, her bikini-clad body soaking up the hot Las Vegas sun. She'd isolated herself with a gossip magazine and a pair of headphones and wasn't aware Logan had approached until his shadow fell across her.

"Hey, Uncle Logan, what are you doing home?"

"I thought I'd take you to lunch and then to meet a woman I know."

The resentful expression she'd had since arriving in town three days ago immediately lifted. She leaned forward eagerly. "I didn't know you were seeing someone. Way to go, Uncle Logan."

"I'm not *seeing* her." The kiss flashed through his mind. "She's just someone who has agreed to show you what running a hotel is like."

"Boring." Madison sagged back against the lounge. "When are you and my parents going to realize that I don't want to be stuck in a stupid office? I want to be an actress."

"Your parents are concerned that you haven't explored all the options available to you."

"Like they want me to explore my options. They want me to go to the college of their choice and major in business or get a law degree and become just like them. It's not what I want."

"I didn't know what I wanted at your age."

She smirked as if he'd just made her point. "That's not true. Mom said you spent all your free time messing with your computers. And you started that security software company by the time you were twenty. You were a multi-millionaire before you even graduated."

"But I still graduated."

"Whatever. The point is, you were successful because you were really good with computers and it's what you loved to do, not because you have a master's in design engineering."

Logan glared at her. No wonder her parents had shipped her off to him. Bringing her into line with "because I said so" wasn't going to work on an intelligent, determined young woman like Madison.

"Fine, but I still graduated from college." He held up a hand when she started to protest. "Face it, kid, for the next month, you're stuck with me and my opinion on what's best for you. Go shower and I'll take you to my favorite restaurant."

Forty minutes later they slid into a booth at Luigi's. Madison stared around her in disgust.

"This is a pizza place."

"Not just any pizza place. They have the best Italian food outside of Italy."

"I thought you were going to take me somewhere nice."

"This is nice."

She rolled her eyes at him. Once they'd ordered, Madison leaned her arms on the table and began to grill him.

"Who is this woman you're dumping me on?"

"Scarlett Fontaine. She runs Fontaine Richesse. You'll like her. She used to be an actress."

Madison's blue eyes narrowed. "Used to be? As in she failed at it, so now she can tell me what a huge mistake I'm making if I don't go to college?"

"Used to be. As in she now she runs a billion-dollar hotel and casino."

And did a pretty good job at it. Or at least she'd hired people who knew what they were doing.

"What is she, fifty?" Madison scoffed. "There's plenty of time for me to come up with a backup plan in case acting doesn't pan out."

"She's thirty-one." It startled him to realize he knew how old she was. And that her next birthday was a month away.

"So young? Why'd she give up so fast?"

"I'm assuming because she was offered the chance of a lifetime."

"Running a hotel?"

"One of Las Vegas's premier hotels."

But Madison looked unconvinced. "She's nothing more than a quitter."

"That's not how I would characterize her."

Forty-five minutes later, they entered Scarlett's hotel and crossed to the elevators that would take them to the executive offices on the third floor. When the doors opened, Logan was startled by the man who stepped out. He and John Malcolm exchanged a quick greeting before the lawyer headed off.

Puzzling over the presence of Tiberius Stone's lawyer in Scarlett's hotel, Logan absently pointed Madison toward the restroom and told her where to find him when she was done. Seconds later, he entered Scarlett's office and caught her sitting behind her desk, full lips pursed, her attention on her computer monitor. Logan noticed immediately that she'd changed her clothes. Now she was wearing a sleeveless lime blouse with a ruffled front that drew attention to her full breasts and showed off her toned arms. She'd left her long hair down and it spilled across her shoulders in a honey-streaked brown curtain that made his fingers itch to slide through it. He sunk the treacherous digits into his pocket and strolled up to her desk.

"I didn't realize you and Tiberius shared a lawyer," he said, skipping a more traditional hello.

She stood up when he spoke. Instinctively he appreciated how the slim black skirt skimmed her lean hips. The outfit was sexy and professional, a delectable one-two punch to his gut.

"We don't." She fetched a manila envelope from her desk. "He brought me this. It's from Tiberius."

"What's in it?"

Surprise flickered in her green eyes at his sharp tone. "I haven't opened it yet. It's probably just something he wrote to say goodbye. He was a great guy. I wasn't as close to him as Violet, but we hung out a lot. He gave me the inside scoop on this town. Who I could trust. Who to watch out for." Abruptly she stopped speaking. Cocked her head. "Why are you so curious?"

"Tiberius collected information on people." Logan wasn't sure how much he wanted to tell her. Damn the wily old man and his insatiable curiosity.

"What sort of information?"

"Secrets."

Her eyes widened. "Dirt?" She turned the envelope over in her hand. When she glanced up and caught his gaze on her, her throaty laugh erupted. "And you think he had something on me." Not a question. A statement. "I'm sorry to disappoint you, but I don't have a closet filled with skeletons just waiting to be exposed." She sobered and leveled a sharp glance his way. "Are you this cynical about everyone or just me?"

"Everyone."

"Not Harper and not Violet." Her tone was mild enough, but accusations shimmered in her eyes. "You trust them."

Meaning, he didn't trust her. Well, he didn't. She was a professional actress whose talent for role play spilled into her personal life. He had a hard time reading her and that made him suspicious of everything she said or did.

"They've never given me a reason not to trust them." His mother would scold him for such a blunt statement. She'd raised both her boys to treat women with gentleness and respect. It was just that Scarlett's wicked eyes and secretive smile got under his skin.

"What have I ever done to you?"

She had him there. His prejudice against her stemmed from the way she affected him. Was it fair to blame her for the way his skin prickled when she brushed against him? Or how the scent of her, light and floral, made his heart slam against his ribs? Or the way his blood flowed hot and carnal through his veins at the sexy sway of her hips as she sauntered through her hotel.

"It's not what you've done." He bit off each word. "It's because you like to play games."

Amusement sparkled in her eyes. "Games can be fun."

Besieged by provocative images of her dressed in black lingerie and thigh-high boots, armed with a riding crop, he swallowed hard. Around the same time she'd shown up in Las Vegas, an episode of a popular crime series had aired. She'd done a guest spot where she'd played the owner of a fantasy club. Ever since he'd seen her on that show, the erotic snapshot had a habit of popping into his head at the most inopportune times.

"I don't play games." Annoyance made his voice gruff.

"Then what would you call that kiss in the elevator?" A challenge flared in her expression. "You kissed me to make a point. How is that not playing games?"

Rather than admit that he'd kissed her because he'd been unable to control his longing to do so, Logan countered with, "What point was I trying to make?"

While Logan awaited her answer with eyebrows raised, Scarlett kicked herself for letting him get to her again. Why couldn't they have a civilized conversation? Okay, she admitted, it was fun to get him all riled up. More so now that she knew that frustrating him led to impulsive kisses. Hot, passionate ones. What would happen if she really exasperated him? Anticipation quivered through her.

She blew out a breath. "That I need a man like you in my life." To her delight, she'd surprised him.

"That's not why I kissed you."

"Sure it is. And I quote—'What you need is a man who

will barge right past your defenses and drive you wild.' Isn't that what you were trying to do when you kissed me?"

Lips tight, he stared at her for a long minute. "I was demonstrating my point, not auditioning for the job."

While her heart hopped wildly in her chest, she gave what she hoped was a nonchalant shrug. "Too bad because you gave a great performance."

Stoic, Logan crossed his arms and indicated the envelope Scarlett held. "Do you know what Tiberius sent you?"

His grave question brought her back to her earlier musings.

"Not yet. Why are you so interested?"

"Lucas thinks Tiberius might have left Violet the files he gathered through the years." Logan shifted his gaze from the envelope to her eyes. "I think he might have left them to you."

"Me?" She glanced at the package in her hand, but her surprise didn't last long. "I suppose that makes sense. We shared a love of Las Vegas history. If his files go back to the fifties, there are probably all sorts of great stories that never made it into the history books." The thought excited her. "It'll make a great addition to my Mob Experience exhibit."

"It's dangerous for you to have those files."

Was that concern turning down Logan's lips and putting a dent in his forehead? She struggled to keep delight from taking over her expression. "Dangerous how?"

"A lot of powerful people have secrets they'd like to keep buried."

This was getting better and better. "I'll bet they would."

He looked none too pleased at her enthusiasm. "Up until now the existence of the files has been nothing but speculation. If anyone gets wind that you have them, someone might decide to come after them." Logan exhaled impatiently. "You might get hurt."

"You're worried about me." Nothing could have prevented her giant smile. "That's so sweet."

He actually growled. "Just because you and I don't get along doesn't mean I want anything bad to happen to you."

"We could get along just fine if you'd stop fighting your feelings for me."

"If you're referring to that kiss in the elevator—"

"That oh-so-steamy kiss in the elevator," she corrected with a smug smile. "And you never did answer my question. Was I acting?"

He regarded her without expression and said nothing.

"Maybe another demonstration would clear up your doubts." She reached out and ran her fingers down his tie.

He snatched her hand in his, eyes blazing. "Damn it, Scarlett."

Before he could complete his thought, a young woman appeared in the doorway. "Hello. I'm Madison."

"Scarlett Fontaine." It was tough taking her eyes off Logan's stormy expression, but she managed. "Nice to meet you," she said, moving out from behind her desk.

"Logan told me all about you."

Amusement twitched Scarlett's lips into a smile. "Really?" She caught his unrelenting gaze and drawled, "*All* about me?"

Logan gave her a tight nod. "I told her that you'd been an actress."

"Not just an actress," she corrected with dramatic flare sure to annoy him. "A star."

"Really?" Now Madison looked interested. "I don't recall seeing you in anything."

Scarlett's smile turned wry. "You probably wouldn't recognize me. I was fifteen when the show ended. But for five crazy years I was Hilary of *That's Our Hilary*."

"I don't think I ever saw that. Have you been on anything since?"

"Guest appearances here and there. A short-running cable show." Scarlett glanced Logan's way and saw that he was scowling at her again. *Honestly.* What had she done now to earn his disfavor? To distract him, she gave him the envelope. "Here, maybe seeing what's inside will keep you from being so cranky."

"Tiberius left it to you." He tried to hand it back, but she shook her head.

"And not knowing what's inside is bugging you, so open it."

With a harsh exhalation, he slipped his finger beneath the envelope flap and pulled out a packet of papers. A key card slipped to the floor. Madison looked curious as she bent to retrieve it.

"It's a rental agreement for a storage unit," Logan said as he continued looking through the stack of papers. He handed a single sheet to Scarlett.

Scarlett recognized Tiberius's neat handwriting. The letter was addressed to her. As she scanned it, her throat tightened. Damn the old rascal. He had indeed passed his files on to her. She took the key from Madison and studied it.

"A storage unit?" she mused. "Do you suppose there's more than files in there?"

"Possibly. I hope you're not considering going there alone."

He might not like her, but that didn't stop him from feeling protective. She could work with that. "Why not?"

His phone chimed, indicating he'd received a text. Pulling it out of his pocket, he checked the screen. Air slipped between his teeth in an impatient exhalation.

"Something's just come up." He turned to Madison. "I'll be back for you at five."

"Five?" Scarlett echoed doubtfully. "The action doesn't get started around here until much later. You just go ahead and do whatever it is you do and I'll make sure Madison gets home."

"What time?"

"I don't know. Midnight?"

Logan's eyebrows dipped as his niece's expression lit up. "Ten," he countered.

"Seriously?" Madison piped up. "I'm seventeen years old. You don't think I've been out past ten before?"

He looked as if he were chewing glass as he countered, "Ten-thirty."

"I'm almost eighteen."

"*Almost* being the operative word."

Madison rolled her eyes at him. "My birthday's two weeks away."

"Ten-thirty."

"When I turn eighteen you can't tell me what to do."

Scarlett watched the exchange with interest, noticing the way his gaze bounced from her to Madison and back. It was good to see that she wasn't the only female who annoyed him.

"Why don't we say eleven," she offered, voice bright, smile friendly.

Her words stopped Madison's revolt in its tracks. "Perfect."

To Scarlett's surprise, Madison moved to her side and linked arms. An unstoppable female phalanx against Logan. He did not looked pleased.

"Eleven." Logan gave a tight nod. "And keep her out of trouble."

"Stop worrying. She'll be fine."

Scarlett gave Logan's authoritative shoulders and don't-mess-with-me stride one final glance as he headed out of her office. Oxygen returned to the room in a rush with his departure. The man sure knew how to dominate a room. And a woman's hormones.

"Let's start our tour in reservations," Scarlett murmured, gesturing the teenager toward the hallway.

"I thought maybe we could begin in the casino."

Scarlett shook her head, crushing Madison's hopeful expression. "We'll save the best for last."

Two hours later Scarlett had shown Madison around the entire hotel and was heading into the casino when her phone rang. Her heart gave a happy little jolt when she recognized Logan's number. *Stupid. Stupid. Stupid.* The man had given her yet another heaping helping of his bad opinion of her today and she still couldn't shake this idiotic crush she had on him.

"I'm a glutton for punishment," she muttered as she answered the call. "Hello, Logan. The tour's going great in case you're worried."

"You're still at the hotel?"

"Where else would I be?" She paused a beat. "Oh, right, the storage unit."

"You're taking this business with the files too lightly."

Scarlett's gaze followed Logan's niece as she ventured toward a display advertising the opening of the Mob Experience exhibit in a month. "I already promised not to take Madison anywhere near the storage unit."

"It's not just Madison's safety I'm talking about."

A warm glow filled her at his concern. "So, when do you want to go check it out?"

"The sooner the better."

"Tomorrow?"

"That should work."

"What time are you going to pick me up?"

She interpreted his hesitation as dismay.

"You misunderstood me," he said. "*I'm* going to check out the storage shed. Alone."

"You could. But you'll have a difficult time getting in without the key." She let her meaning settle in for a couple seconds before she finished, "So, it's a date."

"It's not a date." The vibration in his tone reminded her of an unhappy rottweiler.

"It could be if you took me to dinner first." As she plied him with her most beguiling voice, Scarlett wondered if the sound she was hearing on the other end was his teeth grinding together.

"I'll pick you up at seven."

Scarlett grinned in triumph. "I'll be counting the hours."

First a kiss, now a date. She couldn't believe her incredible luck. Too bad she didn't gamble or she'd be raking in the winnings. Practically floating across the carpet, she caught up with Madison.

"I can't believe how many people are in here," Madison said as they strolled between the tables. "It's three in the afternoon."

"Most people come to Las Vegas to gamble. Wait until later. It'll really be hopping down here then."

"I like the way the dealers are dressed up as famous movie stars."

"My friend Tiberius told me how back in the fifties it was not unusual to walk through the casino and see Lucille Ball, Debbie Reynolds or the Rat Pack. The stars loved coming here." Scarlett paused, wondering if the seventeen-year-old had any idea who she was talking about, and then saw with relief that she did. "Since I grew up in Hollywood, I thought it made sense for me to bring a little of that glamour back to Las Vegas."

"What a fun idea."

It was at that moment that Scarlett remembered Madison was an aspiring actress. "So much fun that I like getting in on the action myself." She linked her arm through Madison's and steered her toward the elevators. "Let's go up to my suite and I'll show you what I mean."

Ten minutes later, Scarlett threw open the doors to her "special" closet and waited for Madison's reaction.

"Cool."

The fifteen-by-fifteen-foot room was lined with costumes, shoes, wigs and jewelry that Scarlett used to transform herself into various starlets from the fifties and sixties.

"On the weekends I like to get dressed up and wander around the casinos. My high rollers love it and I get to pretend that I'm still an actress." A mild pang of regret came and went.

"You obviously love being one." Madison walked toward the costumes on the far wall. "Why'd you give it up?"

Scarlett watched Madison trail her fingers along a hot-pink replica of the gown worn by Marilyn Monroe when she sang "Diamonds Are a Girl's Best Friend" from the 1953 musical *Gentlemen Prefer Blondes*.

"The simple answer is that when puberty hit I went from a sweet-faced girl-next-door to a bombshell with too many curves." Scarlett stood in front of the mirror and gazed critically at her reflection. "Neither the producers of *That's Our Hilary* nor my not-so-loyal public were ready for Hilary to grow up so fast."

"What happened?"

"They spun off a few secondary characters into a new show and gave Hilary the heave-ho."

"That's terrible."

"That's showbiz." Scarlett skimmed her palms over her hips, thinking about how she'd put on the black skirt to thumb her nose at Logan's suggestion that she dress more professionally. He didn't seem to understand that unless she worked really hard to downplay her allure, her innate sexuality came through whatever she wore.

It's why the parts that came her way after her stint as Hilary were all of a kind. She'd turned down so many offers to play sexy roles that she'd lost count. Being typecast as the bitchy sexual rival of the heroine was not the part she wanted to play. She longed to be taken seriously as an actress, but her agent said none of the casting directors he spoke to could see past her looks to the talent beneath.

"I know my uncle wants you to talk me out of being an actress."

"Aren't you a smart girl." Scarlett caught Madison's gaze in the mirror. "Smart enough to have a plan for what happens if you can't make it in Hollywood?"

Madison looked away. "I'm young. I thought I'd give it a few years. If I don't make it, I can always go to school later."

Scarlett considered how many times she'd heard a fellow actor say something similar. It was hard to give up your dream of making it on the silver screen when a great part was always the next audition away.

"Or you could see if your parents would be okay with you attending college in L.A. while you take acting classes and audition." Scarlett could see that Madison hadn't considered this option. She'd probably been so focused on defying her parents and fighting for the future she wanted that she'd never considered there might be a middle ground. "It might be a lot more work than you intended, but it might also be a way to make everyone happy."

"I'll think about it."

But Scarlett could see the teenager wasn't quite ready to.

"In the meantime, do you want to be Judy Garland in *Summer Stock* or Greta Garbo from *Mata Hari?*"

"How about Marilyn?"

Scarlett laughed. "Not so fast, my young apprentice.

First you need to prove to me you've got the chops to be Marilyn."

"I've got the chops."

"Then you won't have any trouble making a casino full of people believe you're Mata Hari."

"You got that right."

# Three

It was ten minutes after eleven, and Logan was pacing from one end of his thirty-foot front porch to the other. There was a pair of rocking chairs where he could sit down and enjoy the flowers cascading from long pots affixed to the railings, but he was too agitated.

Through the Bluetooth receiver in his ear, Logan half listened to his brother muse about Tiberius's files. "So, we were right."

"I'll know for sure tomorrow."

Logan squinted into the dark night as if that could help him see farther. Where the hell were they?

"I don't suppose there's any way she'd just turn the files over to you."

"Not a chance." His irritation spiked as he saw head-lights appear at the end of his long driveway.

"Yeah, I forgot how well you two get along." Lucas sounded disgusted. "I don't know what the hell's the matter with you. She's gorgeous and the chemistry between you is off the charts. You'd barely have to lift a finger to charm the key from her."

"Charming people is your job," Logan retorted, stepping off the porch as Scarlett's Audi TT rolled to a stop. "You're late," he snapped as she cut the engine.

"I'm late?" Lucas said in his ear, tone rising in confusion.

Scarlett protested, "By ten minutes."

"You sound too cranky for this to be a booty call," his brother taunted, having heard the female voice. "I take it our rebellious niece wasn't home on time."

"Something like that. Later." He disconnected the call, cutting off his brother's laughter.

Logan frowned as Madison stepped from the car. "What is she wearing?"

"I'm Greta Garbo as Mata Hari," Madison announced, striking a pose, arms out, face in profile, nose lifted to the sky.

Logan surveyed the elaborate headpiece that concealed Madison's blond hair and the sparkling caftan-looking gown that covered her from chin to toes. With her dramatic makeup and solemn expression, his niece was an acceptable Greta Garbo.

But he'd asked Scarlett to steer Madison away from acting, not demonstrate how much fun it could be.

"Doesn't she look great?" Scarlett asked, coming around the front of the car. Also in costume, adorably feminine in a blond wig and pale pink ostrich-feather dress, she gave Logan the briefest of glances before settling her attention on the teenager.

The fondness in her gaze struck low and hard at Logan's gut. Unprepared for the blow, he stiffened. Scarlett genuinely liked the girl. And from Madison's broad smile and the hint of hero worship in her eyes, the feeling was mutual. When he'd agreed to let Scarlett show his niece around the hotel, he never dreamed they'd become friends. But now he understood his faulty judgment. Having an actress of Scarlett's caliber to learn from would be any fledgling actress's dream come true.

"Just great." He felt a growl building in his chest. "Madison, why don't you go in and take off the costume so Scarlett can take it back to the hotel with her."

Logan's shortness dimmed his niece's high spirits. "She said I could bring it with me when I go back tomorrow."

"I've been thinking that the hotel might not be the best place for you."

"It figures that I'd find something I enjoy and you'd take it away." Madison threw her arms out. "Do you all want me to be miserable? Is that it?"

"I thought you might spend some time with me at the office tomorrow."

"We tried that, remember?" Madison crossed her arms over her chest and dropped the enigmatic Mata Hari facade. Once again she looked like a twenty-first-century teenager playing dress-up. "You left me sitting in the lobby with the receptionist while you dealt with all the supersecret stuff for your clients. No, thanks."

Up until now, Scarlett had remained silent. Now she stepped into the fray, her manner relaxed, her voice a refreshing spring breeze. "Madison, why don't you head in. Your uncle and I will figure something out."

To his amazement, Madison did as she was told. Giving Scarlett a quick, warm hug, his niece shot him a pleading look before disappearing through the front door.

"How did you do that?" The question tumbled out of him. "She fights me on everything from breakfast to bedtime. But you tell her to do something and she agrees without so much as a frown."

"I don't know. Maybe because I've treated her like the intelligent young woman she is."

"Meaning, I haven't?"

"You're pretty bossy."

"She's seventeen."

"When I was seventeen, I had my GED, was managing my acting career and having a ball with my friends."

"She's not you."

"I'm not saying she is. But she's smart and ambitious. If she's behaving like a brat, it might be because no one is listening to her."

"So now you're an expert."

Scarlett's only reaction to his sarcasm was the warning flash in her eyes. Her tone remained neutral as she said, "I'm not an expert. I'm simply offering you my opinion."

"Noted."

"Please let her come back to the hotel tomorrow. She can shadow my general manager. Lucille's exactly what you want in a mentor. A professional career woman with a master's degree in business. Hardworking. Conservative dresser. You'll love her."

While Logan appreciated that Scarlett had taken a strong interest in Madison, he couldn't shake the concern that no matter how hard she tried to steer his niece toward college and a career that would please her parents, Madison would continue to be dazzled by Scarlett's larger-than-life persona and remain steadfast in her decision to become an actress.

"Please, Logan. Let me help." A trace of pleading had entered Scarlett's voice. "I'm worried that if everyone keeps telling her what to do, Madison will become even more determined to skip college and go to L.A."

"And you think you can change her mind."

"I'm not promising that, but I think she'll listen to what I say."

That's exactly what Logan was afraid of. She'd already half convinced him to let Madison return to the hotel. His irritation cooled and other emotions crowded in.

"And who are you supposed to be?" he asked, as he finally took in the full effect of her outfit.

She twirled gracefully. "I'm Ginger Rogers from the movie *Top Hat*."

She looked ready to be spun around the dance floor or clasped in her costar's arms for a passionate moonlit kiss. And thanks to her four-inch heels, her delectable mouth was within easy kissing distance....

Logan crossed his arms over his chest as he was flooded with the memory of her soft moan of surrender earlier that day. A low burn began in his belly. Tension built as he waited for the tiniest spark from her that would ignite him to action.

But instead of provoking him, she retreated a step. "I should be getting back to the hotel."

Did he detect the slightest hint of breathlessness in her voice? Had she sensed he was on the brink of doing something rash and impulsive? Why wasn't she inviting him to act?

"Of course."

"Will you bring Madison by tomorrow?"

"I can."

"It would be better if we formalized the internship by hiring her. That way she can take ownership of the tasks she's assigned."

Logan knew having a job she enjoyed would be good for his niece, but he worried what having her working for Scarlett was going to do to his blood pressure.

"What time do you want her?"

Only because he was so in tune with her did he note the relaxation of her muscles. The change was almost imperceptible.

"Eight."

And then, because she wasn't expecting it, he slid his hand around the back of her neck and lowered his lips to hers. For a second, shock paralyzed her, then she softened beneath the light pressure he exerted on her mouth. The moonlight and muted night sounds called for leisurely, romantic kisses. He cupped her head and focused all his attention on the texture of her plump lips and the fragrance of her skin.

Two kisses stretched into ten. Logan knew the interlude couldn't last forever. Already in the back of his mind irritation buzzed. A sizzling, sultry temptress, she was built for passion and frenzied desire, and here he was treating her like the heroine of a lighthearted romantic comedy.

But in this moment, with just a hint of coolness rushing across his hot skin, he wanted nothing more than to savor the way she yielded her lips to his mastery, to enjoy how her body trembled as he feathered kisses over her chin and cheeks.

"Thank you," she said when at long last he released her.

He noted that she kept her gaze on his shirt buttons, her thoughts hidden beneath a thick fringe of lashes. "For kissing you?"

She frowned. He'd disrupted her poise and she was slow to recover.

"For letting Madison come back to Fontaine Richesse tomorrow."

"You made a convincing argument."

Already his fingers itched to touch her again. He wished he hadn't let her go so soon, but any longer and he'd have been overwhelmed by the urge to carry her into the house and spend the rest of the night ravishing her.

As if reading his mind, Scarlett backed away. "I'd better go." She returned to the driver's side of the red convertible. With the car between them she finally met his gaze. "Are we still on for tomorrow night at seven?"

"I haven't changed my mind about how dangerous Tiberius's files are, so yes."

"Then it's a date."

"It's not a date," he grumbled, but the eager jump in his pulse made him wonder who he was trying to convince, her or himself.

"Then you won't want to kiss me goodnight."

Any response he might have made would've been drowned out by the noise of the engine as she started her car.

It wasn't until her taillights disappeared down his driveway that he realized he was smiling.

The first thing Scarlett did when she returned to her suite was crank up the air conditioning. Driving a sedate forty miles an hour back to the hotel hadn't stirred the hot June night air enough to lower her body temperature after kissing Logan.

She stripped and stepped into the shower. The cool water made her shiver, but it wasn't enough to fully banish the heat coursing through her at the memory of Logan's lips moving over hers.

Somewhat refreshed, she wrapped herself in a terry robe and sat staring out her window at the bright Vegas strip. Why the hell had he kissed her like that? Passion she could handle. That wild kiss in the elevator had knocked her for a loop, but it had been born out of conflict and chemistry.

Tonight's embrace had been heartbreakingly romantic. She never imagined a straightforward guy like Logan would have had it in him to kiss her so sweetly and let her go. The explosive quality between them led her to expect him to want her hard and fast. Not slow and tender.

She felt a quiver begin in her chest and plummet downward until she was just as hot as before her shower.

A firm knock sounded on her outside door, making Scarlett's heart jump. Had Logan followed her back to the hotel intent on picking up where they'd left off in his driveway? If so his timing was terrible. Her hair was wet. She wore no makeup. The only thing sexy about her at the moment was that she was naked beneath the robe.

For several seconds she stood paralyzed with indecision. A second, urgent knock roused her. She crossed to the door and flung it open.

"About time," Violet said, holding up a bottle of Tiberius's favorite Scotch. "It's been a long, horrible day and I need a drink."

"Ditto." Harper eyed Scarlett's attire, then peered past her into the suite. "We're not interrupting anything, are we?"

Scarlett laughed, but it had a queer edge to it. "Hardly. And you're right about the day. It was crazy. I'll get some glasses."

The three sisters settled onto the comfortable couch in Scarlett's living room, each with a glass of amber liquid. Scarlett enjoyed being sandwiched between her sisters, treasured their closeness. Growing up an only child, she'd always longed for siblings. Now she had two.

"To Tiberius," Violet pronounced in solemn tones.

"To Tiberius," Harper and Scarlett echoed as they all clinked glasses.

"How did it go with Logan's niece today?" Harper asked as Scarlett refilled her glass after tossing back the first shot.

The alcohol had left a line of heat from her throat to her stomach, a different sort of burn than she'd felt when Logan had kissed her. "She's great. Wants to be an actress. Her family is horrified."

Violet frowned. "There are far worse professions."

"Not if you listen to Logan," Scarlett muttered. "He's convinced I'm going to corrupt Madison with my evil ways."

"Stop exaggerating." Harper was always the voice of order and reason. "You rub Logan the wrong way because it amuses you."

Scarlett couldn't deny it so she shrugged. "I'd rather rub him the right way, but he made it plain from the start that I wasn't his type."

"Is that why he stares at you so much?" Violet regarded her over the rim of her glass. "Because you're not his type?"

Harper patted Scarlett's hand. "I'm sorry to break it to you, but you're every man's type."

"Not every man." But few were immune. Until today she'd believed Logan was one of those. Correction—until tonight. The kiss earlier that day had been about proving a point. Tonight's kiss had been…intimate. As if the only thing on his mind was connecting with her. Scarlett shook her head and put a stop to such fancy. Turning to Violet, she said, "Something weird happened today. John Malcolm stopped by with an envelope for me from Tiberius."

"Tiberius's lawyer?" Harper sounded perplexed. "What was in it?"

"A key to a storage unit." Scarlet eyed her younger sister. "Did you know that Tiberius kept files on a whole bunch of people?"

Violet shook her head. "What sort of files?"

"From what Logan told me, they're filled with a whole

lot of secrets." Scarlett was still having a hard time taking the whole thing seriously.

"Interesting." Harper leaned forward to look at Violet. "He never mentioned this to you?"

"Not once."

"How do you know all about this?" Harper asked.

"Because Tiberius left me his files." Scarlett nodded when she saw her sisters' surprise and confusion. "Crazy, right? At least that's what Logan thinks is waiting in the storage unit. We're going to go and check it out tomorrow night."

Violet grinned. "You and Logan?"

"Apparently he thinks the files are too dangerous for me to have." Scarlett ignored her younger sister's smug look. "The files are all he's interested in."

"I'm sure." But Violet didn't look the least bit convinced.

"Is it weird that he gave them to you?" Harper asked.

"Maybe." Scarlett rolled her empty glass between her palms. She'd consumed the two drinks too fast. Her head felt light. Her blood hummed through her veins. "Tiberius and I talked a lot about Vegas history. If it wasn't for him I wouldn't be opening the Mob Experience exhibit next month. He gave me the idea, encouraged me to pursue it and most of the items on display were either things he'd collected or were donated by people he knew."

"He loved that you listened to his stories," Violet said. "I was more interested in the future than the past."

"I was fascinated." Scarlett's throat closed up. "He brought Las Vegas to life for me."

Seeing Violet struggling with her sadness, Scarlett wrapped her arm around her sister's shoulder. Five years earlier, when she'd found out she had two half sisters living in Las Vegas, Scarlett had worried they would be angry that she'd been included in Henry's contest to decide who the future CEO of Fontaine Resorts would be. After all, what did she know about running a hotel or a multibillion-dollar corporation? But to her delight, they were as excited about having her in Las Vegas as she was to be there.

"How did it go with your mom today?" Scarlett asked.

"About as you'd expect." Violet offered a wan smile. "She's taking it hard."

Tiberius might not have been Suzanne Allen's first love, but he was her longest and best. Even though she'd never married the hotel owner, she'd lived with him for twenty years.

"Was she any help with the funeral arrangements?" Harper quizzed, dropping her hand over Violet's and giving a sympathetic squeeze.

"You know my mother. She can't make decisions on the best days." Violet gave a wry smile.

"Do you have a date for the funeral?" Scarlett asked.

"Not yet."

Harper frowned. "That's strange."

"Not so strange," Violet said. She heaved a giant sigh. "There's something I haven't told you. There's something suspicious about Tiberius's death."

"Suspicious?" Scarlett echoed, goose bumps popping out on her arms as if someone had touched the back of her neck with an ice cube. Logan's earlier concerns no longer seemed amusing.

Harper looked as worried as Scarlett felt. "I thought he had a heart attack?"

"He did, but they're waiting for some toxicology results to come back from the lab. The investigating officer told Mom they think Tiberius's death might have been from an overdose of digitalis."

# Four

*An overdose of digitalis.*

The words hung in Scarlett's mind as she dressed for her "date" with Logan. It had to be accidental. Anything else was preposterous. Who would want to kill an old man? Someone who had something to hide? She shook off the thought. Logan had put crazy ideas in her head. But she couldn't shake her nerves. And she had lots more than the ticking time bomb Tiberius had left her to worry about. She was about to embark on an entire evening alone with Logan.

Scarlett nearly jumped out of her skin when the knock sounded on her door. She set her lipstick aside and took a breath to settle her racing pulse. Would tonight be all business or would he subject her to another one of those mind-blowing embraces?

There were ways to protect herself from men who wanted to harm her. And where her heart was concerned, Logan had already proven himself a dangerous adversary.

Standing before the door to the hall, she smoothed her palms along her hips. Never had she spent so many hours trying to figure out what a man wanted her to be. In the end, she'd dressed in a pair of skinny black pants and a black blouse with a cap sleeve that bared her arms. With her hair slicked back into a severe bun and tiny pearl earrings as her only jewelry, she was as close to looking professional as she could manage.

Then, because she'd never been good at doing what was expected of her, Scarlett added a pair of heavy black-framed glasses. Now she looked like someone's sexy secretary. Wrestling her features into a bland expression, she opened the door.

Logan's eyes narrowed as he caught sight of her. "What's with the getup?"

She slid the glasses down her nose and peered at him over them. "Don't you think I look professional?"

"You look…fine."

"Fine? I spent all afternoon searching my closet for something to wear so you wouldn't be embarrassed to be seen with me." She couldn't resist the taunt.

"I thought you understood I'm not interested in your playacting."

Scarlett gave him a genuine smile. "Do you really want me to stop?"

"Why wouldn't I?" He gave her a suspicious once-over.

"What happens if you start to like the real me? Where will you be then?" It was a bold sortie, but something about the lick of heat in his eyes told her he wasn't as immune to her as he'd like her to think.

"Why would you think I'd like the real you?"

"Touché," she murmured, unfazed by his question. She intrigued him. That much was clear. He wasn't the sort of man to waste his time if he wasn't interested. For now, that was enough. "I might not be the best-educated or most suited to run a multibillion-dollar hotel business, but I've got my own talent."

"Such as?"

"I do a pretty good job reading people."

"I suppose that's your way of saying you've got me all figured out."

"Not in the least. You've always been a hard nut to crack." She gave him a wry smile. "That's why you're so interesting."

Scarlett grabbed her purse and stepped into the hall. Sharing the space with Logan's broad shoulders and powerful personality stirred up the butterflies in her stomach. Self-protection told her to give him a wide berth, but Scarlett had never been one to run from her fears. Instead, she linked her arm through his and smiled up at him.

"Where are you taking me for dinner?"

"Paul Rubin's new place."

She hummed with pleasure. Romantic and expensive. She never would have guessed Logan had it in him. "I've been dying to try it."

Without commenting, Logan escorted her down the hall. If he'd stuck to his usual pace, Scarlett would have had to trot to keep up. Was he being considerate of her footwear or was whatever weighed on his mind slowing him down?

"Did you know Tiberius's death has been ruled a homicide?" Logan asked when at last they reached the elevator.

"Last night Violet mentioned that the police thought there was something suspicious about his death."

"He overdosed on digitalis."

"Sure, but he was taking that for his heart, right? He just accidentally took too much?" She sounded way too hopeful.

"The digitalis in his system had a different chemical signature than what he was taking. Someone wanted to make it look like an accidental overdose." Logan regarded her dispassionately. "I hope this convinces you how dangerous these files are to have in your possession."

"Your concern is touching." If she gave them up would he remain concerned about her? Scarlett wasn't willing to find out. "But you have no idea why someone killed Tiberius. For all anyone knows, he might have been the victim of a random crime."

"Not random. Someone knew he had a bad heart and wanted to make his death look like natural causes."

"So maybe Tiberius was blackmailing someone. With his death, that stops."

"Unless that person thinks you are going to pick up where he left off."

"I'd never do that."

"I know that, but—"

"You do?" She'd had to interrupt him.

"Of course." He shot her an exasperated glare. "My opinion of you isn't as bad as you think."

"Thank goodness." She sighed in exaggerated relief, earning still more of his displeasure.

"Do you ever stop acting?"

"Only when you're kissing me." She wasn't sure where she found the courage to speak so boldly, but when his eyes widened with surprise, she was delighted she had.

She lifted her chin and offered him her lips but the elevator doors picked that inopportune moment to open. He growled and dragged her inside.

"If there weren't cameras in every inch of this hotel, I'd make you prove that statement," he muttered, jabbing his thumb into the down button.

"We could go back to your place after we check out the storage space," she offered, every inch of her skin tingling where his gaze touched her. Lowering her voice, she whispered, "Unless you've got cameras there for personal use."

Her innuendo was so outrageous that he laughed. "You have a smart-ass remark for everything, don't you?"

"A girl learns to stay on her toes in Hollywood. There are a lot of smart people ready to take advantage if you're not careful."

"Have you told my niece that?"

Scarlett smiled. "She knows."

"How are things going with her?"

"We spent the afternoon at the pool."

"The pool? I thought you understood she's here to learn about hotel management."

"Relax," Scarlett told him. "Every Wednesday I host a fashion show. You know, resort wear, swimsuits. The girls strut around, showing off the clothes we sell at our boutique."

"And what was Madison wearing?"

"I put her in the tiniest bikini I could find. She had men stuffing tens in the itty bit of string that held it together."

Logan drew in an enormous breath, preparing to deliver a lengthy tirade outlining all the reasons Scarlett was unsuitable as a mentor, when he noticed the glint in her eyes. She was teasing him. He shoved his hands into his pockets to keep from strangling her. Or worse. Kissing her.

Her red lips had softened into a slight smile as she watched him. That mouth of hers was going to be his undoing. Whether she was using it to taunt him or yielding to his kisses, he was completely enthralled.

"What was she really doing?"

"I considered putting her in the show, then decided you'd prefer it if I had her emcee the event. She did great. Quite a natural."

Logan knew he should thank Scarlett for demonstrating

some common sense, but anything he said would probably come out wrong.

"She's done a lot of plays and public speaking," he said instead, wondering what he could possibly do to keep this exasperating woman from creeping beneath his skin.

"It shows."

The elevator finally deposited them in the lobby, and Logan escorted Scarlett toward his Escalade parked outside the main entrance.

"You sure like your vehicles big," she commented, stepping nimbly into the front seat.

"And green. It's a hybrid."

"You and Violet." She gave her head a wry shake. "Made for each other."

He shut the passenger door harder than necessary and circled the car. She was right. He and Violet shared a likeminded philosophy about lifestyle and work. So why did it bug him that she kept pointing out the fact? It was either a subtle rejection or a defense mechanism.

Defense mechanism, he decided as he slid behind the wheel. There was nothing remotely subtle about Scarlett.

Which meant she had a reason to feel defensive around him. Interesting.

"Any chance you've talked Madison into going to college this fall?"

"I've had her for a day and a half," she reminded him. "Give me a little time to gain her trust. Then I can start steering her in the direction of school."

"How much time?"

"I don't know. How long is it going to take you to trust me?"

Her question startled him. "I don't know."

"Give me a ballpark."

"I don't know that I ever will."

"There's more of that Wolfe charm." She didn't look the least bit hurt by his reply. "You should package it and sell it on eBay. You'd make a fortune."

Her sarcasm rolled off him like water off a newly waxed car. "Don't ask the sort of questions you won't like the answer to."

"You know what I think?" She prodded his arm. "I think you're going to wake up one day and decide you really like me."

Did anything faze this woman? "What makes you believe that?"

"Call it women's intuition."

"Do you say things like that to annoy me?"

"Most of the time. I love it when you scowl at me. Which is a good thing, since that's all you ever do."

"Why would you like that I find you irritating?"

"Because every other man I meet finds me beautiful and desirable. It gets tiresome. Our relationship is completely adversarial and I appreciate knowing where I stand with you."

"You don't think I find you beautiful and desirable?"

"I guess you might." Her expression lacked its usual guile as she watched him. "But if you do it's secondary to the fact that you don't like me. I find your honesty refreshing."

Only, he wasn't being honest. With her or himself. She disturbed him in a way no other woman had. Which was unfortunate because he didn't trust her and he would never start a relationship, physical or emotional, with a woman who guarded her secrets as closely as Scarlett Fontaine.

By the time Scarlett licked the last of the chocolate from her spoon and set it down on the empty dessert plate, she was convinced she'd never enjoyed a meal so much. Part of her delight had been the delicious food, but most of her pleasure had come from her sullen dinner companion.

Logan had been in a foul mood ever since she'd confessed that she found his honesty refreshing. Why that bothered him, she had no idea. Shouldn't she be the wounded party? He was the one who'd declared he'd never trust her and called her irritating.

"If you wanted dessert," he growled, "you should have ordered your own."

"I just wanted a bite."

"You ate almost all of it." And she knew he'd enjoyed watching her devour the rich treat.

In fact, she wondered if he'd ordered it for just such a reason. From their dinner conversation, she'd learned that he wasn't usually one to indulge his sweet tooth. No dairy. Steamed vegetables. Lean meats. Whole grains. His body was both a fortress and a temple.

"Shall we order another one? This time I won't steal a bite. I promise."

"It's getting late. We need to get to the storage unit." He signaled for the check.

Scarlett was torn. On one hand, she'd love to linger over a cup of coffee and enjoy the thrust and parry of their banter a little longer. On the other, she was tired of having the barrier of the table between them.

Unfortunately, now that dinner was through, the glint faded from Logan's eye and his features hardened into a professional mask. Sighing in resignation, she let him guide her out of the restaurant and into his SUV. With his focus so far away from her, Scarlett knew the only way to reengage with him was to discuss the purpose behind their dinner tonight. "What sort of secrets to you suppose Tiberius had locked up?" she asked, hoping to jostle him out of his thoughts.

"Dangerous ones."

His dark tone gave her the shivers. She studied him as the lights of the Strip faded behind them and they entered an area of town where tourists never ventured. Another man might have played up the seriousness of their outing for effect. That wasn't Logan's style. He was genuinely troubled and Scarlett was less confident with each mile they drove.

"What do you think I should do?"

"Shred the whole mess."

Honestly, did the man not watch TV? "That's not going to help. The killer will assume that I made copies of everything. Or at the very least that I went through all the files and know what Tiberius knew." Whatever that was.

Logan grunted but didn't comment.

By the time they arrived at the storage facility, Scarlett had run the murdered-blackmailer plot from a dozen detective shows through her mind. If Tiberius had been killed because of these files, was she in danger? Her stomach churned, making her regret muscling in on Logan's dessert.

He stopped the SUV in front of Tiberius's storage unit. "Are you okay?" he asked, noting her expression.

"I've played a dead escort and a drowned party girl. I'm not sure I'm ready to play murdered hotel executive."

"This isn't television."

"My point exactly."

Logan took her hands in his and gave them a squeeze. "No one knows you got the files. You're going to be fine."

"This is Las Vegas." She drew courage from his strength and let the heat of his skin warm away her sudden chill. "There are no secrets in this town."

"There are thousands of secrets buried here."

"Did you have to use the word *buried?*"

With one last squeeze, he set her free. "I'll make sure nothing happens to you."

"That's a charming promise, but you're not around 24/7," she reminded him. A smile flirted with her lips. "Unless that's your way of telling me you want to step up our relationship."

His growl helped restore her sense of humor. She slipped out of the passenger seat and waited in front of the storage unit until Logan joined her. With great ceremony she handed him the key to the lock and stood, barely breathing, while he opened the door and raised it. The musty smell that greeted them was similar to that of a used bookstore.

Logan stepped to the wall and switched on the light. "Damn."

The stark overhead bulb revealed two walls lined with four-drawer file cabinets, stretching back fifteen feet. Bankers Boxes sat atop the file cabinets and were clustered on pallets on the floor.

Scarlett whistled. "There are eighty-eight drawers of secrets in there, not to mention what's in the boxes. That's a lot of dirt." She glanced Logan's way and noticed a muscle jumping in his jaw. He hadn't seemed to hear her, so she nudged him. "Were you expecting this much?"

"No. This is worse than I imagined."

"It's going to take us a year to get through all of it."

Logan turned and blocked her view of the files. "Not us. You need to let me deal with this. It's too dangerous for you."

"Tiberius left this to me." His dictatorial manner was a double-edged sword. She liked his concern for her welfare, but she'd left L.A. because she was tired of being told what to do. "You wouldn't even be here if you hadn't shown up just as Tiberius's lawyer was leaving my office." She wasn't trying to make him mad, but he had a knack for bringing out her worst side.

For a second he looked irritated enough to manhandle

her into his SUV and dump her back at the hotel. He still had the key and she doubted her ability to get it back either through manipulation or force. Her best bet was to convince him they needed to work together.

"Two of us will make the search go faster." She took a half step forward, expecting him to back up to maintain his personal space. When he didn't, she splayed her fingers over his rib cage and moved even closer. "Please, can't we work together?"

Beneath her hands, his abs tightened perceptibly, but he stood as if frozen. "There's really no way I can stop you, is there?"

It wasn't exactly an enthusiastic confirmation of their partnership, but she'd take whatever she could get from Logan.

"No, you can't." She gave him a smug smile and pushed back, but his hands came up to cup her arms, just above the elbow, keeping her in place.

"I swear, if anything happens to you because of this…" His mouth settled on hers. Hard. Stealing her gasp and replacing it with the demanding thrust of his tongue. The kiss wasn't calculated or romantic. It was hot, hungry and frantic. Confusion paralyzed her. By the time she recovered enough to react, he'd slid his lips across her cheek. "I would never forgive myself," he murmured in her ear.

He released her so abruptly she wobbled on her four-inch heels. To her immense relief he spun with military precision and marched into the storage unit without a backward glance. The time required to restore her composure was longer than it should have been. But no man had ever kissed her with such hungry desperation. Or rocked her world so fast.

Smoothing her hands down her hips, Scarlett strode toward the files lining the wall opposite from where Logan was searching. The drawers were unmarked, but when she opened the first one, a quick scan of the folders revealed that they were filled with newspaper clippings, handwritten notes, copies of documents and an assortment of photos. A more thorough review indicated each bit of information came from individuals associated with the long-demolished Sands casino.

It seemed as if Tiberius had something on every employee going back to when the casino opened. Not all of it was incriminating. Some of the information merely consisted of impressions he'd recorded upon meeting the person. But there were thick folders on several others, including some legendary performers.

"This is amazing." She turned with a file in her hand. "Tiberius has enough stuff in these files to keep Grady busy for decades."

Grady Daniels was the man Scarlett had hired to help create the Mob Experience exhibit. He lived and breathed the history of Las Vegas. His doctoral thesis had been on the Chicago mobs, but during his research, he'd learned quite a bit about Las Vegas because of the natural migration of mobsters in the forties and fifties.

"Lucas was right," he muttered, either not hearing her or ignoring her enthusiasm. "Tiberius was the J. Edgar Hoover of Vegas."

"You told your brother about the files?"

Logan shook his head. "He told me. We've suspected what Tiberius has been up to for a while." From his guarded expression, there was more he wasn't sharing with her.

Scarlett decided a subtle push was called for. "Finding anything is going to be impossible unless we have some idea what we're looking for. Or a notion of who might have something to hide."

"And we're not going to find anything tonight."

"Give me half an hour to indulge my curiosity, then I'll let you take me back to my suite and have your way with me."

His unfathomable stare told her he wouldn't dignify her flirtation by responding. So with a sigh, Scarlett continued to work her way around the storage unit. She wasn't surprised to find a whole lot of information on the mob, but resisted the urge to take any of the files with her. Some of Tiberius's notes read like pages from an old-time detective novel. The stories were fascinating. Scarlett could easily have spent days in here poring over the metal cabinets, but Logan was showing signs of impatience.

At last she found the file drawer she was looking for. Sure enough, there was a thick file on her father. His antics were well-known around town. Her grandfather's file was not as full as his son's, but it still contained a lot of newspaper articles as well as a history of the company and background on Henry. It took her less than a minute to unearth two other files. One for her mother. One for Violet's. To her surprise, Tiberius had a file on Harper's mother, as well. What could he possibly find of interest about a New York City socialite?

Scarlett shut the final cabinet door and carried her booty to an unmarked Bankers Box near the front of the unit. She thought it was empty until she lifted off the top, but it was a third full of files. From the look of them, these files must have been some of the last Tiberius was working on. She dropped the files on her family into the box and picked it up.

Logan stood outside, radiating impatience as she emerged. "What are those?"

"Files on my family."

"Are you sure taking those is a good idea?"

"Have you met Harper's and Violet's mothers? I'm sure

there's nothing scandalous in their pasts besides our father. As for my mother…" She handed him the box and dug out a photo to show Logan. It was a full-color eight-by-ten photo. "Wasn't she gorgeous?"

"You inherited her legs."

Her pulse stuttered. "You've noticed my legs?"

"It's hard not to."

Unsure whether he meant the comment as praise or mere observation, Scarlett headed toward his SUV without replying. Logan was an enigma. Most of the time he acted as if every second in her company taxed his patience, then suddenly he'd behave as if he was actually worried about her. To further confuse her, he had developed a distracting fondness for kissing her whenever the mood struck him.

He didn't like her. He certainly didn't respect her as a businesswoman. On the other hand, she wasn't his responsibility, so he didn't have to worry about her safety as much as he did. And his kisses…his amazing, confusing, contrary kisses. They certainly weren't the sort a man planted on a woman he was trying to seduce. What was his angle?

Scarlett studied him as he drove back to the hotel. He wasn't classically handsome. More the rough-and-rugged type. Brawny. Take-charge. The guy everyone else in the room deferred to because he had all the answers.

Nor was he a good choice for a woman who only felt safe with men she could wrap around her finger. Was she attracted to the danger he represented? He would break her heart in a millisecond if she gave him the chance. Damn it. It would be so easy if only she didn't like him so much.

Logan glanced her way and caught her staring at him. "What?"

"I was just thinking what a heartbreaker you are."

He snorted. "I think you have us confused."

"I flirt, but I never commit. No one's heart actually gets

engaged. You are completely sincere. You could make a woman fall in love with you without even trying." She angled her body toward him. "Why haven't you gotten married?"

"If this is another one of your games…"

"No game. I'm insatiably curious. I think that's why Tiberius left his files to me." "Knowledge is power," he'd been fond of saying. "Did the right girl never come along?"

"I was engaged once."

Rather than prompt him to continue, she let silence hang between them.

Logan scowled. "She broke it off."

Scarlett shifted her gaze away from his stony expression, wishing she'd left well enough alone. No wonder he was such a hard man to get to know. He'd been hurt by the person who should have loved him best. That wasn't something Logan would let go of easily. Scarlett pitied the women who tried to get close to him. They would find his defenses as impenetrable as the security systems his company was famous for.

"I'm sorry."

"It was ten years ago." He said it as though the pain was a distant memory, but she suspected his wound wasn't all that well healed.

"That doesn't mean it stops hurting."

He greeted her attempt at sympathy with cold silence. At the hotel, per her request he stopped the SUV outside the employee entrance. When he tried to hand the key to her, she shook her head. "Find whatever it is you're looking for."

"Why do you think I'm after something?"

"You don't really expect me to believe you came along tonight because you enjoy my company." Managing a light-hearted smile despite the heaviness in her chest, Scarlett exited the vehicle and lifted the box containing her family's files from the backseat.

"Scarlett…"

"Keep in touch, Logan."

Then, before she could make the mistake of asking him up to her suite, she shut the car door and headed toward the hotel's employee entrance.

# Five

A week went by before Logan admitted defeat regarding Tiberius's files. Scarlett had been right. Someone could spend decades going through the fragments of data. The hotel and casino owner had accumulated thousands of interesting tidbits throughout the years, some of it newspaper articles, some rumors, many firsthand accounts of events that had never become public knowledge.

The problem was, there was so much information, most of it random, that connecting the dots would take forever. Logan had neither the time nor the patience to locate the needle in the haystack. If he'd had some idea what he was looking for, he might have been able to ferret out Tiberius's killer. But although the files held a lot of smoking guns, many of the people who'd once held them were long dead.

Nor were the cops interested in looking through the files. They were looking at the wife of a local businessman. Apparently the woman had been having an affair and after finding a file on her at his office, the police had a theory that Tiberius was blackmailing her. Logan didn't believe it. Tiberius collected information on people, but he didn't appear to use it. If he had, the casino owner wouldn't have been nearly bankrupt when he died.

Despite having no luck, giving up the hunt was the last thing he wanted to do, but Scarlett was eager to have her historian comb through the files in search of material they could use in her Mob Experience exhibit, which was due to open in a few weeks. He could have given the key to one of his guys to return. In fact, that would have made a lot more sense. He was hip-deep in the data Lucas had sent to him from Dubai. They needed to have a proposal done in the next couple days and he'd lost a lot of time in his search through the storage unit.

Instead of leaving the key with Scarlett's assistant, a stunning blonde woman with an MBA from Harvard, he tracked Scarlett herself down on the casino floor. He found her chatting with one of the pit bosses. With her hair cascading down the back of her sleeveless bronze sheath, she looked every inch a successful hotel executive. His chest tightened as he watched her smile. Seven days away from her should have diminished his troublesome attraction. Instead, he'd found his thoughts filled with her at the most inopportune times.

Desiring her had been his Achilles' heel for some time now, but he'd been able to keep his head in the game by remembering that she was first and foremost an actress and a woman who enjoyed manipulating men. Until last week, however, he'd never spent an extended time alone with her. He'd been working off assumptions he'd made from their infrequent encounters.

He now knew she was more than the manipulative maneater he'd first dubbed her as. Not that this made her any less dangerous. Quite the contrary. His fascination with her had ratcheted up significantly. And not all of it was sexual. He'd enjoyed her company at dinner. She was provocative and took great pleasure in testing his boundaries, but she was also very well-read and had surprised him with her knowledge of Las Vegas past and present.

She was more clever and insightful than he'd thus far given her credit for. She knew her limitations and had a knack for hiring people who were experts in their field. It's why her hotel was so well run, he'd decided after eight days of listening to Madison go on and on about how smart Scarlett was. For the first couple of days his niece's hero worship had worried him. But Madison hadn't mentioned L.A. once in the past several days, and he was happy to let her praise Scarlett's virtues if it meant his niece was going to give college a try.

"Hello, Logan." Scarlett had finished her business with the pit boss and caught sight of him. "Are you looking for Madison?"

"No." He held his ground against the onslaught of sensation that battered him as she drew close enough for him to smell her perfume and see the gold shards sparking in her green eyes. "I came to return this." He handed her an envelope containing the storage key.

"You're done with it, then?" She slid the envelope into the black leather folder that contained her daily notes. "Did you find what you needed?"

"I looked through our client's files and removed anything of interest." He paused before saying more. Lucas would be angry with him for spilling even that much. "I also found a number of secrets that should never see the light of day."

"Then they won't."

"You can't guarantee that."

"Some of those files have been hidden for over fifty years," she reminded him. "What makes you think they can't stay that way for another fifty?"

"Because Tiberius was killed for something he knew."

"That hasn't yet been determined. Besides, no one but you and I know I have the files."

"You forget about John Malcolm."

"Attorney-client privilege. He's not going to say anything."

"I'd feel better if the files were destroyed."

"I can't do that. Grady can't wait to get started on them."

Logan could hear the determination in her tone and knew he was wasting his breath. He could only hope he and Lucas were wrong about the connection between the files and Tiberius's death. Yet Logan couldn't shake the sense that something bad was going to happen.

"Do you have time for a cup of tea?" Her offer came at him out of the blue. "I got some of that green stuff you and Violet drink."

He opened his mouth to refuse, thinking she was flirting with him as always, but then saw her expression was serious. "Sure."

"Can I invite you up to my suite without you getting the wrong impression?"

"Unlikely."

"What a naughty mind you have." Amusement flared in her eyes and was gone just as fast. "I really could use your advice." She looped her arm through his and turned him in the direction of the elevators.

A week ago he might have assumed she had a nefarious purpose for luring him upstairs. That was before Tiberius's files had come to light. And Scarlett was radiating an apprehensive vibe, not a seductive one.

"My advice on what?"

"I discovered something in the files I took from the storage unit, and I'm not sure how to handle it."

Logan felt his anxiety kick in. Had she possessed the answer to Tiberius's murder all along?

"Which ones?"

She frowned. "The ones on my family."

So her concern was for Violet or Harper. His agitation diminished slightly.

"I took my father's file because I was curious about a man my mother rarely talked about," she continued. "It was a pretty thick file and took me three days to get through it all. He had affairs with a lot of women. I don't know how Harper's mother stood it."

"The way I understand it, she split all her time between New York City, the Hamptons and their winter place in Boca Raton. I don't know how often she came to Las Vegas."

"That's what I gathered from her file." Scarlett paused as they neared the elevator. Other people were waiting within earshot and she obviously didn't want them to overhear her, so she changed the subject. "How was your week? Successful?"

He knew she was referring to his search of the storage unit and shook his head. "Not at all. Your friend is going to have his work cut out for him. There's a lot of history."

"He'll be delighted."

"I'm sorry I didn't call this week." The apology came out before he knew what he was saying. "It was a hectic few days."

Surprise fogged her expression for a moment. "It's okay. I had a lot on my plate, as well."

"Lucas and I are developing a security system for a sheikh in Dubai. He has an extensive art collection that he wants to display and the logistics are proving quite complex."

She watched him with lively interest as he spoke. "Sounds fascinating," she murmured.

When the couple riding in the elevator with them got off on the twelfth floor, the snug space seemed to shrink.

"I don't know about that, but it is challenging." It wasn't like him to fill the silence with chitchat, but her open and sincere manner made him long to draw her into his arms and capture her lips with his. This frequent and increasing urge to kiss her was becoming troublesome. To his relief, the elevator door slid open on fifteen before he could act.

"I'd love to learn more about what it is Wolfe Security does besides casino security." And to her credit, she seemed to mean it.

"Perhaps another time." And there would be another time, he realized. She'd found a way beneath his skin and he feared it was only a matter of time before she took up permanent residence there and started redecorating. "Right now, I'd like to hear about what you found in Ross's file."

She waved her leather portfolio near her door's lock. All the rooms in Fontaine Richesse used proximity cards to open rather than ones with magnetic strips. The radio frequency in the cards was a harder technology to copy. Logan had been suggesting it for use in Fontaine hotels for three years as a more effective security measure, but none of the executives wanted to upgrade. Until Scarlett came along and decided it was the system she wanted in Fontaine Richesse. Now, all of the new Fontaine hotels had this system and as the older hotels were being remodeled, proximity card systems were being added.

Before she entered her suite, she gripped his arm. "Logan, I'm really afraid of what this is going to do to my family."

He stared at her, a bad feeling churning in his gut. This wasn't Scarlett being dramatic or overreacting. Genuine fear clouded her expression and thickened her voice. What could possibly have upset her to this extent?

"Tell me."

She entered her suite and headed for the kitchen. "I'll get the water started. The files are on the table." Scarlett indicated a stack of neatly arranged folders on the coffee table. "I noticed something odd about my father's business travel."

Logan sat on the pale green couch, noting its decadent softness, and leaned forward to view the contents of the open file. Tiberius had jotted some notes about Fontaine Hotels and Resorts's trouble with their Macao casinos. Ross had gone to investigate.

"What am I looking at?"

"See when he left? July 1980. He was gone for four months."

Logan shook his head, not understanding what Scarlett was getting at. "What's the significance of that?"

"Harper was born in June 1981." She raised her voice over the scream of the teakettle. "Now look at Penelope's file."

Penelope was Harper's mother. The only daughter of billionaire Merle Sutton, whose fortune revolved around chemicals and refining, her marriage to Ross Fontaine had brought an influx of cash to Fontaine Hotels and Resorts at a time when, unbeknownst to his father, Ross had bought some land without the proper environmental surveys. Ultimately, they'd been unable to develop the property and lost several million on the project.

Logan opened the file and scanned a private investigator's report on Harper's mother. Below it were several black-and-white photos that left little to the imagination.

"She had an affair." He stared at the pictures and felt

a stab of sympathy for the woman who'd been part of her father's business arrangement with Ross Fontaine. "Given the man she was married to, I can't say I blame her."

"At first I thought Ross had ordered the investigation." Scarlett carried two steaming cups over to the couch and set them down on the coffee table before sitting beside him. "I thought it was a little hypocritical of him to have Harper's mom investigated when he went after anything in a skirt. But it wasn't him."

"You sure?" Logan glanced sideways in time to see her lips close over the edge of the cup. "How's the tea?"

The face she made at him caused her nose to wrinkle in a charming manner. "It tastes like dead grass." But she gamely tried a second sip. "I checked on the private investigator." Scarlett pointed to the man's name on the report. "He's been dead for ten years, but his partner didn't find Ross's name in their list of former clients."

"Was it Tiberius?"

Scarlett shook her head. "Of course, Ross could have been considering divorce and gone to a lawyer who contacted a PI to get evidence of Penelope's infidelity. But once he got proof, why not start divorce proceedings? Then there's this." Scarlett opened a second file and showed Logan a document. "Harper's parents were not in the same hemisphere when she was conceived."

"She might have been conceived during a brief visit either in Macao or here in the States."

"I agree, but coupled with the fact that Harper's mother was having an affair during that time, it seems much more likely that this guy—" she tapped the photo "—is Harper's father."

Scarlett scrutinized Logan's impassive expression while she waited for him to process her conclusion. When she'd found the damning evidence last night, she'd longed to pick up the phone and share the burden with him, but it had been three in the morning and she hadn't wanted to wake him up.

Loneliness had never been an issue for her. In L.A. when she wasn't busy with friends, she'd enjoyed spending time alone. It was one of the benefits of growing up an only child. But lately she'd been dreading her own company. Sharing the secret of Tiberius's files with Logan had turned their animosity into camaraderie and their temporary break in hostility was something she wanted to make permanent.

"Which brings me back to why I invited you up here," she said, breaking the silence when it began nibbling on her nerves. "What should I do?"

"What do you want to do?"

She decided not to answer his question directly. "If I do nothing, Harper will become the next CEO of Fontaine Hotels and Resorts."

Logan sat back and stretched his arm across the back of the sofa. The move put his fingers very close to her bare upper arm and made her skin tingle.

"After your father died and before your grandfather came up with his contest to run the company, she was the obvious choice."

Scarlett pondered his words. "She has the education and the training to be Grandfather's successor. But Violet has the marketing savvy and the experience of running a Las Vegas hotel to give Harper a run for her money."

"If you share what you know, Harper would likely be kicked out of the running and the contest would be down to you and Violet."

"That's not what I want."

"You don't want to run Fontaine Hotels?"

Could she convince Logan that having two sisters who

loved her was more important than becoming CEO of a multibillion-dollar corporation?

"You and I both know I'm a distant third in the running. And even if I wasn't, I would never want to win if it meant hurting either Harper or Violet."

"Then you have your answer."

"But I keep asking myself, if I was Harper would I want to know I was living a lie? When I was first contacted by Grandfather, I was angry with my mother for evading the truth about my biological father. I don't know that it's fair to put Harper through the same thing."

"On the other hand, if you'd never found out, you would still be in L.A."

"Finding out I was a Fontaine was a wonderful thing. I gained an entire family that I'd previously known nothing about." Having two sisters was such a blessing. For the first time in her life she felt safe and content. "If I tell Harper the truth, she loses her entire family. And I know her well enough to be certain she would withdraw from the contest and give up Fontaine Ciel. And if that happened it would be my fault."

"What if her dream isn't running Fontaine Hotels?"

Scarlett couldn't imagine such a thing. "It's what she's spent her whole life training for."

"Just because you think your life is going to go a certain way doesn't always mean that it's the best thing for you."

What was Logan trying to tell her? She'd invited him up here for advice. Was he being impartial, trying to get her to look at both sides, or was he couching his opinion as questions?

"Do you think I should tell her?"

"What do you want to do?"

"Give the problem to someone else." She arched her eyebrows. "Feel like being the bearer of bad news?"

"I'm not going to get involved. Tiberius left the files to you."

"And I asked you to help me make a decision."

"You asked for my advice," he corrected.

"Same thing."

"Not really, but since you asked so nicely, I'll tell you that I think being honest with Harper is the way to go. Give her the file, don't tell her what's in it and let her make up her own mind about what she finds."

His advice didn't make the weight slide off her shoulders. "I don't want to keep anything important from Harper. And I could be jumping to conclusions. It's completely possible that Harper is Ross's daughter." But deep in her heart she believed she was right and that telling her sister what she suspected would do more harm than good. "You've given me a lot to think about." She set her hand on his. "Thank you."

For a few seconds he went still beneath her touch. Before she had time to register the way his mouth tightened, he was on his feet.

"I've got a bunch of work waiting for me back at the office," he said. "Thanks for the tea."

"You didn't drink any of it." He'd almost reached her front door by the time she'd regained her wits and chased after him. "Logan." She didn't reach him in time to stop him from walking out the door, but her breathless voice made him pause. "Would you have dinner with me tomorrow night?"

His refusal came through loud and clear before the words left his lips. "I don't think that's a good idea."

She was ready for his rebuff. "Oh, not like that." She plastered on a lively grin and laughed. "You certainly have a high opinion of yourself, don't you?" To her relief, he looked surprised by her reaction. Conceited man. He really expected her to take his rejection hard. "I thought we could discuss what to do for Madison's birthday party. She's only going to turn eighteen once and without her parents here to celebrate with her, I thought we should do something special to mark the occasion."

"What did you have in mind?"

"Have dinner with me tomorrow and I'll lay it all out for you."

"Can't you tell me now?"

"I don't have my notes and I need to get ready for a conference call in half an hour. How about eight o'clock tomorrow? I'll get us a table at Chez Roberto."

"Eight."

He nodded curtly, but when she expected him to walk away, he didn't. She stopped breathing while she waited for him to move or speak. His intense gaze trailed over her features before locking on her mouth.

A thousand times this past week she'd relived his kisses. Like some silly teenager she'd tried to guess how he felt about her when logic counseled it was nothing but simple lust. Hadn't his absence this week demonstrated his lack of interest? When men wanted her, she received flowers, offers of dinner or, at the very least, phone calls. From Logan: nothing.

And it was driving her crazy.

Which is why she'd concocted the excuse for tomorrow's dinner. She was perfectly capable of arranging a fabulous birthday party for Madison by herself. In fact, everything was already handled. She just wanted to spend more time with Logan. And she'd take him any way she could get him.

To her surprise, he cupped her head in his palm and dragged his thumb across her cheek. Mesmerized by the contact, she grabbed the door frame to steady herself as he leaned down and captured her lips in a demanding kiss. Before her shock faded, he lifted his mouth from hers.

"Eight," he repeated, voice and expression impassive. A heartbeat later he strode off down the hall, leaving a weak-kneed, much-bemused Scarlett in his wake.

He'd done it again. Logan strode into his house and threw his car keys on the counter. He was utterly incapable of a clean getaway. He'd nearly made it out of Scarlett's suite when she'd stopped him. He should have given her some excuse and gotten out of there. Instead he'd lingered and agreed to have dinner with her again. And why? So they could discuss plans for Madison's birthday party. He suspected she had the whole thing planned already. This was just an excuse to torment him over another rich chocolate dessert.

And he'd agreed. As if he hadn't guessed what she was up to. Worse, he'd then succumbed to the urge to kiss her again. Demonstrating once more that she'd completely mesmerized him. She no longer had to stir him up with her sharp wit and sexy smiles. Now he just took any excuse to seize her delectable lips for his own.

Madison was seated on the couch in the family room as Logan walked past. Beside her was the boy she'd been seeing a great deal of, Trent something, the son of one of Scarlett's restaurant managers. She'd been instrumental in introducing the teenagers, which had naturally made Logan suspicious of the boy. But a phone call to one of his employees had provided the sort of information on Trent that kept Logan from getting overprotective.

Currently they were joined at the hip and shoulder, both peering at the laptop balanced on the boy's lap. Madison's happy smile was the first he'd seen in this house. It lifted his spirits.

"Hi, Uncle Logan."

"Hello, Madison. Trent." Logan gave the boy a friendly nod. "Madison, are you planning on sticking around for dinner?"

"Yes. Is it okay if Trent joins us?"

"The more the merrier."

Logan left them and headed to the master bedroom. As badly as he wanted to know what they were looking at on the computer, he left his question unasked. The boy was a good kid. Spending time with him improved Madison's attitude.

And all the credit belonged to Scarlett. Instead of lecturing the eighteen-year-old about what would be the best thing for her to do, Scarlett had talked with her. Let Madison express her dreams and ambitions and found a way to broach the topic of college in a positive fashion. By introducing her to kids her own age who were college-bound and excited about it, Madison had started talking about college again. Granted, with little enthusiasm, but he shouldn't expect miracles.

If Scarlett actually pulled this off, he would owe her a favor. The thought of it made him shudder. What would she ask in return? Something difficult for him to deliver, no doubt.

After a half hour of energetic laps in the pool, he showered and headed back toward the kitchen. To his amusement, Madison had chosen to host her new friend in the dining room. She'd had his housekeeper, Mrs. Sanchez, set the table with all the crystal and fine china. Usually, Logan grabbed a plate and headed into his study to work on whatever he'd left hanging throughout the day. When Madison was home, he made an effort to give her a stable family experience and ate in the kitchen. He couldn't remember the last time he'd used his dining room.

Logan sat down at the head of the table and waited only until the teenagers had joined him before launching into his interrogation.

"Madison tells me you are going to be a sophomore next fall," he said to Trent, determined to get his money's worth out of his housekeeper's roast beef with garlic mashed potatoes and steamed asparagus. "What college do you attend?"

"I'm at Duke."

Logan turned to Madison. "Didn't your mother tell me you'd gotten into Duke?" Maybe she liked this boy well enough to follow him to college in North Carolina. Her parents would be thrilled.

"Yes." She leveled a warning stare at him. "I also got into Brown University, Cornell and Mother's alma mater, Amherst." All prestigious East Coast schools.

"Wow." Trent gaped at her in astonishment. Apparently she hadn't shared her academic triumphs with him. "That's impressive."

"I guess." She was so obviously glum about it that for the first time Logan felt sorry for her.

"You guess?" Trent asked. "I applied to Brown and Cornell and couldn't get in."

She had the grace to look a little ashamed of her attitude. "All I mean is that none of those were schools I wanted to get into. I didn't get into my top choice."

This was the first he'd heard of a college she hadn't been able to get into. Was that why she'd been acting out all spring? Paula and Ran had pushed hard to get her to apply to schools they considered suitable. Madison's two older brothers were at Harvard and Yale, respectively. Could she have felt too much pressure?

"What school could possibly have turned you down?"

Logan held very still, hoping that Madison would forget he was sitting across from her and keep talking. He might be able to get her back on track if he understood why she derailed.

Madison waved one slender hand. Her expression had gone mulish again. "It doesn't matter. I didn't get in and I have no interest in going to any school my parents badgered me into applying to."

Trent was smart enough to realize he'd hit a nerve and rather than continue to pursue what was obviously a touchy subject, he stuffed a forkful of Mrs. Sanchez's excellent food into his mouth and chewed with relish. Madison pushed beef around her plate and seemed preoccupied with her thoughts.

Logan applied himself to his own dinner and pondered what he'd learned tonight. Madison wasn't opposed to going to college, she just didn't want to go to any of the ones her parents had encouraged her to apply for. And she'd been disappointed after putting all her hopes in one basket and losing out.

Perhaps if Paula and Ran could let Madison make her own choice about where she went, she could be college-bound in the fall. He would call Paula and talk it over with her in the morning.

Scarlett sat on the overstuffed chair in her bedroom, her feet tucked beneath her, and stared out the window. While Harper and Violet had chosen to occupy suites that over-looked the Strip, Scarlett preferred a view of the mountains that circled Las Vegas. During the cooler months, she enjoyed hiking the trails in nearby Red Rock Park. The peace and quiet was a nice change from the constant activity around the hotel.

It was an hour before she was supposed to meet Logan for dinner, and she still needed to jump in the shower and get ready. She'd finished her day at six so she could get back to her suite and have plenty of time to prepare, but she'd spent the past hour sitting and daydreaming.

No. That wasn't true. She was waiting. Waiting for Logan to call and cancel their date.

She glanced at the clock on her nightstand and frowned. Surely he wasn't the sort of man to stand a girl up at the last minute. He was far too honorable for that. Her stomach gave a queer lurch. Was it possible he wasn't going to cancel on her? Scarlett jumped to her feet. She only had an hour to get ready. What had she been thinking to wait so long?

Her cell rang as she reached the bathroom door. If she didn't answer Logan's call, was their date officially canceled? She shuffled back to the dresser she'd passed and scooped up the phone. To her relief, it wasn't Logan.

"Bobby," she exclaimed. She hadn't spoken with the television producer in over six months. "What a lovely surprise."

"Scarlett, L.A. misses you." Over the phone Bobby Mc-Dermott came across as staccato and abrupt, but in person, he was a warmhearted teddy bear. "You must come home."

Her heart twisted in fond melancholy, but she kept her voice light. "Las Vegas is home these days."

"Bah. You're an actress, not a hotel manager."

"I used to be an actress." She thought back over yesterday's conversation with Logan. "At least when I got work, which wasn't often."

"You are a wonderful actress. You just weren't getting offered the right parts."

She couldn't argue with him there. What she wouldn't have given for a role with some meat. Something that scared her a little and forced her to stretch. She'd never been a fame hound, although with her sex appeal and early success, she was well-known to the gossip magazines and paparazzi.

"That's why I'm calling," Bobby continued. "I have something you'd be perfect for."

Scarlett sighed. She'd heard that before. Bobby had brought her numerous opportunities, but his opinion of her talent always seemed to clash with those of his directors. Still, it was nice having someone of his stature in her corner even if she never did get the part.

"I'm really happy here, Bobby."

"Nonsense. You're an actress. You need to act." The producer switched tacks. "At least come to L.A. and take a meeting."

"There's no point. I'm committed to staying here and managing the hotel." She didn't explain about her grandfather's contest or the pride she felt for all she'd accomplished in the past five years. "You're a darling for thinking of me, though."

"I'm going to send you the script," Bobby continued, ignoring her refusal. When he had his mind set on something, it took an act of God for him to change direction. "Don't make any decisions until you've read it through."

Knowing it was dangerous to open the door even a crack, she nevertheless heard herself say, "I'd be happy to give it a read. But I can't promise anything."

"You will once you've finished. Gotta run. Love you."

She barely had a chance to say goodbye before Bobby hung up. Stewing in a disorderly mash of dread and excitement, Scarlett quickly showered and dressed. At seven forty-five, a knock sounded on her door. Her hair was still up in hot rollers and she hadn't finished applying her makeup. Cursing Logan's early arrival, Scarlett quickly stripped out the rollers and shook out her hair. A second knock sounded on her door, this one more insistent, and she raced to answer it.

"You're early," she declared as she threw open the door.

But instead of Logan, a man in a ski mask stood at her door. "Who—?"

Before she could finish, his fist connected with her jaw. She saw stars. Then darkness.

# Six

With each hour that passed, Logan found himself growing more impatient for the evening ahead. By the time six-thirty rolled around he was positively surly, or at least that's what his executive assistant had called him. Then Madison had complained about his bad temper when he'd arrived home.

Now, as he negotiated the eastbound traffic back to Fontaine Richesse, his mood perked up alarmingly. Damn it. He was looking forward to spending the evening with her. To seeing what sort of delectable outfit she'd prepared for him. To letting her steal food off his plate and wheedle out of him intimate details about his life. Why had he agreed to have dinner with her? He should have insisted on meeting her at her office during the regular workday when he wouldn't be tempted to linger for a nightcap in her suite.

A nightcap that might lead him to forget how quickly she turned on the charm. He would find himself seducing her and believing it was his idea. He'd have her naked and writhing beneath him before he realized she'd orchestrated the entire event. He simply couldn't let her manipulate him that way.

By the time he arrived at Fontaine Richesse, he was running five minutes late. He dialed Scarlett's cell, but she didn't pick up. That was odd. She was rarely beyond arm's reach of her phone. Driven by an irresistible sense of urgency, Logan's pace quickened as he made his way through the casino. By the time the elevator deposited him on Scarlett's floor, he was deeply concerned at her lack of response.

Rounding the corner to her suite, he noticed the door was wide-open. When he spied her on the floor, he ran the rest of the way down the hall. He entered her suite just as she lifted a hand to her jaw and opened her eyes. He knelt at her side as she groaned in discomfort.

"What happened?" he demanded, his throat constricting as he surveyed her for damage.

"I answered the door and a man hit me." She sounded bewildered and weak.

"What did he look like?"

"He was wearing a ski mask." She blinked in disbelief. "All I remember is that his hand shot out. Then everything went black."

"How long ago?" Logan dialed the Fontaine Richesse's security office.

"It was quarter to eight. Someone knocked. I thought it was you at the door." Her gaze found his. "I was mad at you for showing up early. My hair wasn't done and I hadn't finished putting on my makeup."

"You look beautiful," he told her brusquely.

A voice came on the line and Logan quickly outlined what had happened. Security would call the police and get working on tracking the guy who'd broken in. A man in a black windbreaker and jeans would be a challenge to find in a hotel as large as Richesse.

As soon as he hung up, he scooped Scarlett into his arms and headed toward her bedroom.

"No!" She tugged at his suit coat to get his attention. "Not in there…"

"I'm not planning on taking advantage of you."

"I had trouble deciding what to wear tonight, so…" She stared at him, her green eyes dazed. "Logan Wolfe, did you just make a joke?"

He raised his eyebrows in answer. "Where would you like me to put you down?"

"The couch would be fine. And then if you wouldn't mind getting me the package of lima beans that's in the freezer."

"Lima beans?" He eased her down on the sofa and settled a pillow behind her head.

"I happen to like lima beans."

"No one likes lima beans."

"Not even someone as health-conscious as you?"

"Not even me." He brought her the package of frozen beans and gently applied it to her bruised jaw. "Where's your ibuprofen?"

"In the kitchen cabinet to the right of the sink."

He fetched the pills and brought her a glass of water. Her gaze tracked his movements as warily as a cat watching a large dog who'd invaded her territory. Snatching a throw off a nearby chair, he spread it over her legs. A part of him realized he was fussing over her, but he needed to act. And since charging out into the night in search of her assailant wasn't an option, seeing to her comfort made him feel as if he was accomplishing something.

"Nothing in here looks disturbed. Do you keep your valuables locked away?"

"I have a safe for my jewelry. There really isn't much else of value here." She glanced toward the dining room table. "The files."

He followed her gaze. "The ones you took from the storage unit?" From where he stood he could see that the box was still on the table, but the number of files looked smaller. "Some are missing."

"Which ones?"

She swung her feet off the sofa and started getting to her feet. Before she'd fully straightened, her body swayed. Logan caught her around the waist and drew her against him. Her head found his shoulder as she leaned more fully into him.

"Slow down." He should have immediately deposited her back on the couch, but the feel of her, soft and yielding against him, was too appealing. His palm rode her strong spine up and down.

"I have to know which ones are missing. What if the information about Harper gets out? I need to tell her what I discovered."

"Nothing can be done about that at this second. You were hit hard enough to black out. I think you should go to the hospital."

"There's no need for that."

Before Logan could argue further, a hard knock sounded on her door.

"Sit. We'll discuss the hospital as soon as you make a report to security and the police."

"I'm not going."

Grinding his teeth at her stubbornness, Logan resettled Scarlett on the sofa and went to let in Security.

By the time she'd given her statement and her suite had been dusted for prints, Scarlett's agitation had reached an acute stage. Logan's presence calmed her anxiety at having her privacy so roughly violated. The package of frozen lima beans had helped numb her jaw, but nothing could ease her worry over the missing files.

The thief had taken the files for Harper and her mother, Scarlett and their grandfather. In addition, although she hadn't yet looked through the files that had originally been in the box, Scarlett thought two of those might be missing, as well.

"I really couldn't have gotten through this without you," she told Logan after he'd walked the uniformed officers to the door.

"You needed me. I was here."

And now she sensed he wished he were elsewhere. Whether to chase down the man who'd stolen the files or just to be on his way, Scarlett wasn't sure.

"I suppose you need to get home."

Inwardly she cringed at the obvious reluctance in her voice. Sure, he'd been acting solicitous and protective, but that was how he'd treat any damsel in distress. She shouldn't take it personally. No matter how wonderful it felt to have him hold her in his arms and treat her as if she were made of the finest porcelain.

"I called Madison to let her know where I was and sent one of my guys over to keep an eye on her."

"I'm sure she'll love that," Scarlett retorted, her skeptical tone masking her need to snuggle against his powerful chest and take comfort from the strength of his arms around her. For such a hard, unyielding man, he'd demonstrated he could also be gentle. She found the combination both calmed and excited her.

"He'll watch the house from the road. She'll never know."

His somber words caused her uneasiness to spike. "Do you think she's in danger?"

"No." The single word came out too fast and too sharp.

Scarlett didn't find his frown reassuring. "I don't believe you."

"Until we know what's going on, I prefer not to take chances."

"We should probably let Violet and Harper know what happened."

"Already done." He'd been busy while she'd been telling her story to the police. "They will call you tomorrow."

"I guess there's nothing left for me to do, then." Her statement hung in the air between them. She needed him to stay but couldn't bring herself to admit it. Huddling deeper into the throw wrapped around her shoulders, she waited for him to leave.

"I don't think it's a good idea for you to remain here alone tonight."

Her stomach flipped. Usually he was no more willing to offer his help than she was likely to ask for it. The change in his attitude made him more dangerous than a hundred ski-mask-wearing intruders.

"I'm sure I'll be fine if I don't invite anyone in." She tried to compel her lips into a reassuring smile but couldn't.

Logan assessed her and his expression grew more determined. "Nevertheless, I'm going to stay."

She'd already let him take control of the situation. In fact, she'd enjoyed having him in charge. But letting him know how desperate she was for his company could give him the advantage in the future.

"Fine," she said, her manner grudging. "I don't have the energy to kick you out anyway."

His lips quirked. "You're welcome."

"The guest room is made up if you want to use that for what's left of the night."

"The couch will be fine."

"Because you don't want to get too comfortable in my suite?"

"Because if anyone is getting back in, they're coming through that door." He gestured over his shoulder toward the door to the hallway.

Scarlett shivered. The idea that the robber might come back was unnerving. Suddenly it was hard for her to breathe. She began to feel dizzy and set her forehead against her knees. A quiver passed through her as the anxiety she'd bottled up these past couple of hours refused to stay contained a second longer.

"Scarlett." Logan knelt beside her. His large hand was warm and reassuring against her shoulder. "Are you okay?"

"I'm fine." She sat up straight and dashed away the wetness on her cheek.

He exhaled impatiently. "Will you stop trying to act like nothing is wrong when it's obvious you're upset?"

"Of course I'm upset." She let her temper flare. It terrified her to let down her guard around him. "Shouldn't I be? I was attacked and whatever the thief took tonight might have damaging consequences for my family."

"Right now what you need is sleep." He held out his hand.

His suggestion made sense, but she didn't move. It was far nicer to be in the same room where she could be comforted by his reassuring strength. But telling him that would give him too much insight into how she thought.

"You're sending me to bed?" She let him pull her up and forced a mocking smile. "Most men would be escorting me there." -

"Then most men are jerks for taking advantage of you in such a vulnerable state."

Vulnerable? If that's how he saw her, she'd given far too much away tonight. "Most men can't help themselves. They find me irresistible."

"That's a pretty powerful feeling for you, isn't it?"

She set her hand on her hip, a trace of spunk returning. "What's wrong with feeling powerful?"

"Not a thing. Unless you have to be that way all the time."

"I don't." But she was lying. Being strong was how she'd survived being a child star and how she'd struggled back from the dark years of partying too much and falling once too often for the wrong guy. "There's nothing that I can do right in your eyes, is there?"

She turned away before the longing to throw herself at him grew too strong to resist. Her feet felt heavy and sluggish as she crossed the living room. With each step she took, her heartbeat slowed. She hoped he'd come after her, sweep her into his arms and carry her the rest of the way to her bed. When that didn't happen, she closed her bedroom door and left a trail of clothes to mark her passage. Naked, she fell into bed.

But the weariness that dragged on her limbs didn't reach her mind. Scarlett lay on her back, staring at the ceiling, and turned the theft of the files over and over in her head. Had the thief taken them without seeing what they were because he was in a hurry? Or had he broken in specifically because he wanted something that was in them?

She'd gone through her family's files a dozen times. The only damaging item was the fact that Harper's father wasn't Ross Fontaine, and Scarlett couldn't imagine Penelope hiring someone to steal the files. It had to be something else. What had she missed?

Closing her eyes, Scarlett sifted through the contents of her father's file, but all she got for her efforts was an increased throbbing in her head. Ross had been a rotten husband, but that wasn't exactly a huge secret. He'd preferred his women young and single so there weren't any jealous husbands. And he'd been more ham-fisted than ruthless in running Fontaine Hotels and Resorts to have made any enemies among the other hotel owners in Las Vegas.

Scarlett just couldn't see why the guy had wanted the files. And then she recalled the rest of what was in the box. Caught up in the drama surrounding her family, she'd only glanced through the other files once.

Most of the material had been about Tiberius's brother-in-law, Preston Rhodes, the current chairman of the board and CEO of Stone Properties, which was headquartered in Miami, Florida. Like Fontaine Hotels and Resorts, Stone Properties owned hotel and resort properties all over the world.

Scarlett had once asked Tiberius why he didn't work for the company his father had founded and learned how his brother-in-law had schemed to get Tiberius kicked out of the family business so he could take over.

No surprise, then, that Preston had never set foot in Las Vegas. Stone Properties had one hotel on the Strip: Titanium. Run by JT Stone, Tiberius's nephew and namesake, the five-star hotel sat several blocks north of the trio of Fontaine hotels.

An hour ticked by, bringing her no closer to sleep. Logan's presence in the living room was far too distracting. At last she got up and slipped into a hot-pink cotton lounge set. She stood with her hand on the doorknob for a few minutes, debating what excuse she'd use for wanting his company. In the end it didn't matter because when she reached the living room, Logan was nowhere to be found.

Her disappointment was difficult to ignore as she headed into the kitchen for a bottle of water. Instead of drinking it, she set the cool bottle against her still-aching jaw. The coolness washed through her and without warning, tears sprang to her eyes. Normally she'd blink them away and shove down her unhappiness. *Never show weakness.* She'd learned that early in Hollywood. But being abandoned by Logan was too much on top of everything else she'd gone through tonight.

As the tears began working their way down her cheeks, the door to her suite opened. Heart pounding in sudden alarm, Scarlett was too overcome by panic to move. When Logan stepped into view, she was awash in relief.

"You came back."

His gaze swung in her direction. "I never left."

"You weren't here when I came to get water."

"I stepped outside to talk to Lucas." He gestured with his cell phone. "I didn't want to disturb you." As he spoke, he narrowed the distance between them. "Is your jaw still sore?"

He'd moved within reach and before she could question the wisdom of her actions, Scarlett pressed herself against his strong body. She wrapped her arms around his waist and felt him tense. But when his hands touched her shoulders, it wasn't to push her away but to gather her still closer.

"Don't worry," he said. "You're safe."

And for the first time in a long time, she knew she was. Letting someone take care of her wasn't comfortable for Scarlett. She'd developed a deep and wide streak of distrust not long after reaching puberty. The older brother of one of her fellow actors had cornered her in a dressing room and stuck his tongue down her throat. Afterward he'd threatened to say she'd come on to him if she told anyone what had happened. She'd been twelve years old at the time and was just beginning to understand what it meant to be a woman.

"I'm not always strong," she told him, her voice muffled against his shoulder. "Usually I'm terrified that what I'm doing is completely wrong."

Logan stroked her hair. "You've sure fooled me."

"That was the idea."

Logan drew Scarlett toward the couch. They sat together in the middle with little space between them. Scarlett snuggled against his side and her lips curved into a dreamy smile when his arm came around her shoulder. It was a serene, domestic moment, unlike their normally tempestuous encounters. The invasion of her home had cracked her shell, knocking her off her game.

For the first time he didn't question whether this was honest fear or just a performance to make him sympathetic toward her. He'd seen her acting range. She could transform herself into whatever played into a man's fantasy. Since he'd criticized the way she dressed, he'd noticed her wardrobe had become more professional. Was she donning another costume, one designed to win him over? Did she even comprehend what she was doing? Or was it second nature to her?

"You're a hard woman to read, Scarlett Fontaine."

Tonight, she'd been as rattled as he'd ever seen her. So much so she couldn't bring herself to tell him she was afraid.

Her sigh brushed his neck. "I hate to admit it, but you bring out the worst in me."

He was silent a long moment. "Why is that?" He asked the question, not expecting she'd tell him the truth.

"I guess I want too much for you to like me."

Her declaration caught him off guard. Had she recovered her equilibrium? Was this an act? She'd been prickly when he'd told her he wasn't going to take advantage of her. She hadn't appreciated his chivalry. And she'd been right to say that few men would've let her go to bed alone. Sitting alone out here with nothing but an unlocked door between them was a harsh test of his willpower.

"Why do you care what I think?"

"Because I like you and I know you don't approve of me."

He couldn't believe what he was hearing. "Why do you care what I think?"

"There aren't a lot of people who don't like me." She huffed out a small laugh. "I know how that sounds, but I've always had a knack for winning people over."

"I've seen you in action many times."

"I can hear it in your voice. You don't approve of how I behave." She sounded grumpy.

Against his better judgment, Logan found her dismay charming. "Does it occur to you how ridiculous it sounds to say you want me to like you when you've been provocative and difficult at every turn?"

"I'm simply responding to your scorn." She flashed him a baleful glance. "Call it self-preservation."

Hadn't he been just as guilty of provoking her? "Should we call a truce?"

"And have you lose interest in me because things become boring between us?" Her green eyes had regained some of their wicked sparkle. "Half the reason you find me so attractive is because I keep you guessing."

"You're sure I find you attractive?"

He'd no sooner uttered the challenge when her hand curved across his thigh. His muscles twitched in response and her lips arced impishly. That she was touching him to prove a point was the only thing that kept him from flipping her onto her back.

"If you knew all my secrets," she said, "you'd find me deadly dull."

"I can't imagine that's possible."

To hell with his earlier stance on not taking advantage of her in a vulnerable state. There was only so much temptation a man could take. And the pressure behind his zipper demanded that he give up the fight.

He bent down and captured her mouth in a slow kiss meant to satisfy his need for deeper intimacy with her. She moaned beneath his lips and twisted her body until she was sliding backward. Unwilling to be parted from her even for a second, Logan broke off the kiss and scooped his hands beneath her ass, repositioning her with her spine flat on the couch, his weight crushing her into its soft cushions.

"Are you okay?" he asked noticing her slight wince. He pushed a hair away from her face and eyed the spot where the intruder had hit her. "If your jaw is hurting, we should stop."

"Don't worry about it."

Logan wasn't convinced. "You've swelled up a bit where he hit you."

"I'm fine."

"Really?"

"Just shut up and kiss me."

As fierce as his desire was for her, Logan wasn't about to rush the moment he'd been fantasizing about for weeks. No matter how deeply lust sank its talons into his groin, he intended to explore every inch of her skin, taste each sigh, absorb the entirety of her surrender.

He applied gentle kisses to her parted lips, causing her to murmur in encouragement. With his weight pinning her, she had little hope of wiggling and driving him mad with provocative movements, but her hands were free and she used them to her advantage.

After ruffling his hair and tracing his spine, she tightened her grasp on his shirt and pulled it free of his pants. Braced against the first touch of her skin against his, he kept up the slow seduction with his lips and tongue. She sighed as her palms connected with his lower back. Logan couldn't prevent the instinctive twitch his body gave as she raked her long nails up his sides.

Ignoring the heat blazing between them, he cupped her cheek and licked at her lips, running his tongue along her teeth before flicking her tongue. Beneath his palm he felt her facial muscles shift and knew she was smiling. He kissed her nose, a grin of his own blooming at her heartfelt sigh.

"Why so impatient?" he teased, taking her plump lower lip between his teeth and sucking ever so lightly.

Her nails bit into his back. "Because five years of foreplay is too long."

"Five years?" Carefully avoiding her bruised jaw, he nuzzled the soft skin below her ear, inhaling her smooth, fresh perfume and the sharper tang of her earlier stress. If nothing else reinforced his need to take his time, this reminder of what she'd been through tonight did. "Is that what we've been doing all this time?"

"Of course." She adjusted the angle of her head to grant him better access to her neck.

"How do you figure?"

"You don't seriously think all that animosity between us was anything other than frustrated sexual energy, do you?"

He knew what it had been on his part, but was surprised she admitted to being similarly afflicted. "Are you saying you've wanted me this whole time?"

He tried to make his voice sound shocked, but ended up

fighting a groan as she found a way to free her left leg from beneath him. By bending her knee, she was able to shift his hips into the perfect V between her thighs. Her intimate heat pressed against his hip even through the layers of fabric between them. Breath rasping in and out of his lungs, he held perfectly still to savor the sensation.

"Of course."

He believed her because whenever they touched, the walls tumbled down between them. And in this place where they communicated truth as easily with words as they did with their bodies, he was in serious danger of falling hard.

Was that why he'd doubted and taunted her all these years? Because he suspected that if they had a civil conversation he might have to face just how crazy he was about her? All her flaws became insignificant. All his misgivings seemed to be paranoia.

"Make love to me, Logan," she pleaded when the silence dragged on too long. "Don't make me wait any longer."

"I want nothing more," he admitted. "But let's take it slow."

"Slow?" She didn't look happy.

"Slow," he confirmed. "You're worth savoring. Relax." He reclaimed her lips and soothed her with soft, romantic kisses. "We have all night."

Scarlett put her impatience aside and let Logan set the pace. The ache between her thighs didn't abate, but neither did it intensify as they exchanged a series of slow, sweet kisses. The give-and-take of his lips against hers was comforting and the fog of desire dissipated from her mind, offering her a chance to enjoy the feel of his strong body where it pressed against hers and the subtle cologne he'd applied for their date tonight. She concentrated on relaxing her muscles, ignoring the hunger needling her. Logan was right. They'd waited this long. Why rush it?

His kisses did unexpected things to her emotions. Lighter than soap bubbles, joy pushed outward from her center. Logan made her feel like no other man ever had. Cherished. Appreciated. Understood. The excitement she'd expected to feel as his body mastered hers was tempered by the need to relish every second of their time together.

"Why are you smiling?" Logan asked, drifting his lips across her eyelids and down her nose.

"I've never necked on the couch like this."

"Never?" Surprise peppered Logan's question. "I find that hard to believe."

"It's true. Necking is something you do with your boyfriend on your parents' couch or in the back of your boyfriend's car."

"Seems to me you had both a boyfriend and access to a couch and car."

"I wasn't a normal teenager. For one thing, I didn't go to regular school. I had tutors and studied between scenes. For another, my boyfriend at the time liked partying with friends and hitting the club." Not kicking back and hanging out alone with his girlfriend.

"Oh, right, you were dating that boy-band reject back then."

Hearing Logan's derision, Scarlett wished she'd kept her mouth shut, but now that the door was open, she might as well step through.

"We started dating when we were fifteen." Lost in girlish, idealistic fantasies about love, she'd relished their role as America's sweethearts, but their private interaction wasn't nearly as romantic as their public one. "After being fired from *That's Our Hilary* because my image was becoming too sexy and getting offered nothing but vampy bad-girl parts, I tried to clean up my image by trotting out this vow of chastity until I got married." The armies of paparazzi following them had eaten it up. Reacting the way any normal eighteen-year-old boy would, Will had dumped her.

"You're a virgin?" Logan did a lousy job hiding his amusement behind mock surprise.

"Don't be absurd." To punish him, she rotated her hips and rubbed her pelvis against his erection. His eyes glazed with satisfying swiftness. "After Will and I broke up, I discovered celibacy wasn't all it was cracked up to be."

"So, you've never necked on a couch before," he prompted. "Anything else I should know about?"

Too much. But those things would have to wait until she had a better handle on what was happening between them. "One revelation per day is all you're going to get."

"At this rate, it'll take the rest of my life getting to know you."

His offhand remark created a vacuum between them. Scarlett kept her eyes lidded and her breath even as she said, "It never occurred to me that you'd let it take that long. You're so impatient when it comes to getting answers."

"Some things are worth waiting for."

It wasn't like Logan to be cryptic, but Scarlett had no chance to question him further. His lips returned to hers with more intensity, and she knew the time had come for serious play between them.

When she'd dressed in the lounge suit, she hadn't planned on Logan's strong, sure hands smoothing over her curves, but now she was glad she hadn't slipped into her underwear first. As bare beneath the hot-pink fabric as the day she was born, Scarlett knew the instant Logan's fingers discovered her secret.

"Scarlett," he groaned her name as her nipple tightened against his palm. "What you do to me."

She arched her back and bared her throat for his lips and tongue. After working her into an unsteady mess, he glided his mouth across her collarbone and deposited gentle kisses in the hollow of her shoulder. His chin nudged along the edge of the fabric as he dusted his lips across her breast-bone and worked his way toward her cleavage.

The zipper of her lounge suit surrendered beneath the downward pressure of Logan's fingers. She gasped as cool air washed across her bare skin, but his lips skimmed over her ribs, warming her once more. Desire rushed through her as Logan finished unfastening the jacket and laved her quivering stomach. Sensation lanced straight to her hot core, leaving her head spinning.

Impatience clawed at her, but the man refused to move at the speed she so desperately craved. Now, instead of kissing her lips and neck, he was paying entirely too much attention to her abdomen, rib cage and the ticklish spot just above her hipbone.

"Logan, there are other parts of me that are hungry for your attention." She tugged on his shirt, urging him to stop ignoring her breasts.

"Are there, now?" He kissed his way upward. "And what might those be?"

"My breasts are feeling very lonely." She gathered them in her hands and offered him their aching fullness.

With a smile he licked around one nipple. "They are so beautiful, I was saving them for later."

She was half-mad with the anticipation of having his mouth so close but just out of reach. "Not later," she insisted as his tongue flicked one sensitive button. "Now."

"Whatever you say."

She had never imagined that ordering him to do what

she wanted would be so thrilling. A moan ripped from her throat as he pulled her nipple into his mouth and sucked. Scarlett sank her fingers into his thick black hair and held on tight as an ocean swell of pleasure pushed her out of her depths.

"More," she ordered as he switched to her other breast. "I need more."

He soothed her with a single word. "Soon."

But her need for him was escalating too fast and they both had too many clothes on. She grabbed ahold of his belt and tugged to get his attention. "This has to go."

Unable to budge him, she hooked her fingers in the waistband of her own pants and eased them downward, knowing she couldn't get them off but hoping he'd get the hint and help her.

"Not yet."

But as he reached down to tug her hand away, she turned the tables on him and pulled his fingers across her mound.

"Yes," she purred, parting her thighs still farther to encourage him to explore. She was rewarded by the slide of his finger against her moist heat. "Right there."

Throwing her head back, she closed her eyes and centered every bit of concentration on the swirl of Logan's tongue around her breast and the drag of his fingers at her core. She could feel tension invade his muscles and knew what he'd hoped to prolong was moving forward at its own speed, gaining momentum as it swept them toward their ultimate destination.

Her own body was tightening pleasurably. A smile curved her lips as she once again felt the downward drift of Logan's mouth on her body. This time he didn't linger at her stomach, but continued to move at a torturously slow pace to the place where she burned.

* * *

Logan eased her pants down her thighs. Blood pumped vigorously through his veins, clouding his vision. He blinked, needing desperately to focus on the exquisite body he was slowly baring—the large, full breasts, tiny waist and flat stomach. The jut of her hipbones and those long, toned legs. Absolutely gorgeous. And all his.

Tossing her pants aside, he settled between her thighs and cupped her round butt in his palms. Her eyes flew open as he set his tongue against her and drank in her essence. As demanding as she'd been a moment earlier, she melted like butter beneath his intimate kisses now. Her fingers clutched at his shirt, gripping hard enough to tear the seams.

He opened his eyes and watched her come apart. As she surged toward completion he experienced a rush of gratitude that he was here, giving her this pleasure. Her mouth opened as her entire body stiffened. His name escaped her in a keening cry.

As she drifted back to earth, he sat up and stripped off his clothes. He pulled a condom out of his wallet and sheathed himself. Any hope of taking his time was smashed by her parted thighs and welcoming arms. He lay back down, and angled his hips until the tip of his erection sat at her entrance. Her arms closed about his neck, her fingers playing with his hair.

"I need to feel you inside me," she murmured, kissing his chin.

He dipped his head and kissed her soft lips, the contact tender and slow. When her tongue stole out to mate with his, he slipped into her in one smooth stroke and groaned. She clasped him in a snug embrace and the sensation was too much for words. But one stood out in his mind.

"Amazing."

"Absolutely."

Moving inside her was the single most incredible thing he'd ever experienced. Somehow she knew exactly how to shift her hips to achieve the ideal friction. Making love on the couch wasn't ideal, but their shared laughter as they jostled for leverage and strained to pleasure each other with lips, hands and movements made the moment completely perfect and totally theirs.

He'd never imagined feeling such a strong connection with any woman, much less the one who'd been a thorn in his side for five years. Maybe she was right. It had been simple sexual frustration. Once they satisfied their itch for each other, they could go politely on their way, never to take jabs at each other again.

Somehow the idea that he might never get another night with Scarlett filled him with anguish. He kissed her hard, grappling with the notion that his desire for her could ever be fully slaked. But if she continued to drive him crazy, what did that mean for the future?

He quickened his pace as control abandoned him. Scarlett matched his intensity, her expression tight with concentration as they drove together toward completion. As she began to peak, her eyes opened and locked on his. The smile that emerged on her passion-bruised lips speared straight into his heart. It wasn't carnal or greedy in nature. It was heartbreakingly open. She'd offered him a glimpse into her soul and it was brimming with optimism and hope.

Logan buried his face in her neck to escape what he'd seen, but the image haunted him as he felt her body begin to vibrate. The bite of Scarlett's nails against his back triggered his own orgasm. Muscles quivering, nerves pulsing with frantic energy, he thrust hard into her and let himself go. Together they crested, voices blending in perfect harmony.

Bodies trembling in the aftermath, they clung to each

other. Logan's chest pumped, drawing much-needed air into his lungs. Scarlett's fingertips moved languidly up and down his spine, her touch soothing.

Damn. What the hell had just happened?

"Give me a second and I'll move," he muttered, his voice raw and shaken. He hoped she would credit the workout they'd just had for causing him to sound so unsteady. She couldn't find out how his feelings for her had deepened until he could sort out what to do about it.

"Take your time." Scarlett's voice was maddeningly relaxed and calm. "I'm enjoying the feel of all this brawn."

While his heart thumped hard enough to break a rib, Logan kissed her cheek and the corner of her mouth. "Why are you smiling?"

"Are you kidding?" She laughed. "When was the last time you tore someone's clothes off and had sex on a couch?" Her finger dug into his ribs. "And don't you dare tell me last week."

"I did not tear your clothes off."

"No," she agreed. "You took way too much time removing them." She framed his face with her hands and forced his gaze to hers. "Are you okay?"

"I'm the guy," he reminded her, turning his head so he could kiss her palm. "I'm the one who's supposed to ask that."

She twitched her shoulders. "So ask."

"Are you okay?"

"Never better."

Logan kissed her lips. "You know, we really should get off this couch."

"Don't you dare." Her arm wrapped around his neck, holding him in a tight vise. "I like it right here."

"At least let me…" He shifted his weight off her and lay on his back, pinning her on her side between him and the back of the couch. "That's better," he said, pulling the conveniently placed throw over their naked, cooling bodies.

"It's nice."

With her cheek resting on his shoulder and her body a curvy miracle half-draped over him, Logan closed his eyes and wondered when he'd enjoyed such contentment. Usually he was a burn-the-candle-at-both-ends kind of guy. He spent most of his days overseeing his company's massive operations here in Las Vegas and his evenings dreaming up better technology to keep his clients' assets safe.

Taking time for a personal life had been a low priority. Sure, he dated. A guy had needs. But he wasn't one to linger after a nice dinner and some satisfying sex. He never exactly bolted for the door, but he certainly didn't stick around long enough to snuggle.

This experience with Scarlett was much different. He was at peace. Delighted to hold her in his arms until the sun came up, watching her sleep or talking. Was it crazy that they argued about everything but blended seamlessly the instant they kissed? Would their differing points of view eventually taint their lovemaking?

It was no surprise that Logan was already thinking in terms of endings. Didn't he enter every relationship with an eye on how and when it would end? Perhaps it wasn't fair to the women he saw that he perceived their time together as finite, but his perspective was realistic. Even nine-year relationships ended. That his fiancée could choose her career over him had struck a devastating blow. One he wasn't going to let happen again.

And he needed to be more wary than ever because slipping into sleep beside him was the first woman since Elle who had the potential to catch him off guard.

# Seven

Humming happily, Scarlett dived into the clear, cool water of the private pool located on the same floor as her private suite. She loved to swim, and tried to spend at least thirty minutes in the morning doing laps. If she had a little more time, she floated across the dappled surface and enjoyed the lush vegetation planted around the pool deck.

She ached in all sorts of muscles this morning. Making love on a couch was just the sort of thing she might have expected from Logan. Waking up to his soft kisses and hard erection had been a nice surprise. If she'd been asked to bet how he'd behave in the cold light of a Las Vegas dawn, she would have put her money on him returning to his impatient, bad-tempered self. And she would have lost every cent.

Not only did he wake up aroused. He was playful in the morning. And unexpectedly romantic. For a woman who was used to being treated like some sort of trophy, Logan's willingness to make her coffee and feed her orange slices had given her hope that she wasn't simply a conquest.

Her happy glow persisted through the rest of the morning. At noon she headed to her office, where reality intruded. The script Bobby had promised to send sat in the middle of her desk. She tore open the package and scanned the short note he'd included. Even though she'd already decided against auditioning, there was no stopping the excitement that rushed through her. New scripts meant new opportunities and so few had come her way in the past few years.

Although she had no intention of returning to Hollywood and told herself it was foolish to get worked up about the project, she cleared her afternoon schedule and read the entire script twice. The writing was really good. The story fresh and daring. It was the exact thing she'd longed to do, but no one would give her a chance.

Almost as if on cue, as soon as she completed her second pass, her cell rang. It was Bobby. She set the pages aside.

"Well?" He sounded confident and smug as if he already knew what her reaction would be. "Aren't you perfect?"

"I don't know if I'm perfect," she hedged, struggling to keep enthusiasm out of her voice. "But it's a wonderful script and it's going to be a great show."

"Then you'll come and test?"

Here was where she had to face reality. "I really can't. I live in Las Vegas now. I'm responsible for this hotel. I can't just abandon everything and run off to L.A. because of a great part." Besides, there was no guarantee that she'd get the role, and being rejected for something so perfect for her would be a devastating blow.

"The director's an old friend of yours."

"Who'd you get?"

"Chase Reynolds."

Damn. As fabulous as Chase was in front of the camera, the former actor had proven himself to be even more worthy behind it. "He'll do a great job."

"So will you."

"Bobby…" Her tone had taken on a desperate note.

"Gotta run, Scarlett. I'll be in touch later this week."

The call ended before she could protest further. Scarlett's head fell back. The ceiling became a blank canvas for her thoughts. She wouldn't be the first actor to live outside of Hollywood and practice her trade. But how many of those had a demanding position as executive manager of a hotel? Not that she was all that hands-on. She'd hired the right people for key jobs and was little more than a figurehead. Wasn't that how Logan perceived her?

Logan.

Now that they'd taken things to the next level, this was a terrible time for her to be away from him. But she'd never let a man stand in the way of her career before. Of course, she'd never had a man like Logan Wolfe either. And keeping him there was worth a little sacrifice. A little sacrifice, maybe, but this was a fabulous part in a groundbreaking new show. A show that could give her career an enormous boost.

If she still wanted a career as an actress. Did she?

Scarlett surged to her feet and exited her office. In the excitement of getting the script, she'd almost forgotten the other pressing problem facing her. That of telling Violet and Harper that Tiberius had accumulated files on them. And that those files had been stolen. She'd start with Violet. See how that encounter went. Perhaps she'd even pick her half sister's brain about the best way to approach Harper. As well as how much to tell her.

After letting her assistant know where she'd be, Scarlett headed to the walkway that would take her to Fontaine

Chic. She sent Violet a quick text to find out where they could meet up and followed that with a call to Madison.

"I'm sorry to make this so last-minute," Scarlett said to the young actress wannabe, "but I'm going to have to cancel dinner tonight. In fact, why don't you take the rest of the night off."

"Are you sure?"

"Weren't you telling me something about a party one of your friends was having?"

Concerned that Madison wasn't spending enough time with kids her own age, Scarlett had arranged for her to meet some college-bound teenagers that Logan couldn't help but approve of. Sensible kids from good families, they were keen to start at their various schools in the fall, and Madison had caught some of their enthusiasm. Another couple weeks with them and Logan's niece would be ready to resume an academic path.

"Trent is having a few friends over."

"Then you should go. You've worked hard all week. Time to have a little fun."

"I'll tell Uncle Logan that you said that."

Scarlett winced. As amazing as last night had been, she wasn't sure Logan would appreciate hearing her make suggestions about his niece's social life. "Oh, please don't."

"Why not? He really likes you."

"He does?" Scarlett had reached Fontaine Chic and her steps slowed.

"Sure. Just like you have a thing for him."

Why fight it? "I have a huge thing for your uncle. And we're just starting to get along. I don't want to risk annoying him."

Madison laughed. "After the way he was smiling this morning, I don't think you have to worry about it. See you tomorrow."

Left to muse over Logan's good humor, Scarlett didn't even notice she'd passed by Violet until her sister grabbed her arm and gave her a shake.

"You were certainly miles away," Violet said with a curious smile. "Thinking of anyone in particular?"

Scarlett felt the jolt all the way to her toes. Was Violet fishing? There was no way she could know what Scarlett and Logan had been up to the night before. Nevertheless, a guilty flush crept up her chest.

"Nothing like that."

"Look at your poor jaw." Violet murmured, abruptly sober. "How bad is it?"

"I'll survive." Scarlett brushed off her sister's concern. "But the incident last night is why I need to talk to you."

"Sounds serious."

"Let's go to your office so we won't be disturbed."

"That's the worst place we could go. How about we head to Lalique?"

The centerpiece of Violet's hotel was an enormous three-story crystal chandelier that enclosed an elegant two-story bar in dazzling, sparkling ropes. It was three million dollars' worth of *oh, wow* and set the tone for her decor. Like the sky-blue in Harper's Fontaine Ciel, crystal was Violet's signature. Multifaceted and ever-changing, clear crystals sparkled above the gaming tables and from the fixtures that lined the walkways. Pillars sparkled with embedded lights made to resemble crystals and all the waitstaff and dealers wore rhinestone-accented black uniforms.

Settling into a quiet corner table, Violet ordered two glasses of sparkling water with lime and an olive pâté appetizer to share. She then turned to her sister.

"Something is obviously bothering you," Violet commented.

Scarlett gathered a large breath and began. "I told you how Tiberius had left me his files."

"Yes. Have you had a chance to dig into any of them?" Violet's eyes were bright with interest. "What kind of dirt did he have on people?"

"I haven't had time to look at more than a couple." This was the part that was tough. "There were files on our father and you, Harper and me."

Violet didn't look surprised. "I can only imagine what he dug up about Ross." Unlike Scarlett, Violet had known from an early age that she was Ross Fontaine's illegitimate daughter. She'd never had any contact with him, but was pretty sure he knew he was her father. That he'd refused to acknowledge her had been hard on Violet.

"Quite a lot. But none of it was that damning. I mean, we all know he was a philandering jerk, but mostly Tiberius was interested in keeping an eye on his running of Fontaine Hotels and Resorts."

"So the reason you're upset has nothing to do with Ross?"

"Not directly."

"Spill it."

"The files were stolen last night."

"That's what the thief was after?"

"I don't know for sure. He took other files as well. Ones that had nothing to do with us. Tiberius was keeping an eye on his brother-in-law. Almost half the box was filled with stuff on Stone Properties. Financials. Their employees. I just glanced at it."

Violet nodded. "Tiberius hated Preston for the way he treated his sister. Blamed him for her death."

Scarlett's pulse jerked. "Why is that?"

"Preston's priority was the company he took over after his father-in-law died. He wasn't much of a father or a husband. Unfortunately, Fiona Stone adored her husband and couldn't handle his neglect. She turned to drugs and alcohol to cope and died of an overdose when JT was about twelve."

JT Stone ran the family's operations in Las Vegas. A handsome, enigmatic businessman, he didn't socialize with the Fontaine sisters, but Violet had gotten to know him a little because he was Tiberius's nephew.

"How awful to lose his mom so young," Scarlett said, thinking of all the substance abuse she'd seen ruin lives during her years in Hollywood. "Anyway, in addition to those files, the guy grabbed the files Tiberius had on all of us." Scarlett noticed Violet wasn't at all surprised. "You knew?"

"I suspected." She grinned. "Anything interesting?"

Scarlett felt a little of her dread ease. "There was a great deal on my time in L.A. Nothing too shocking there. I kept the paparazzi busy for several years during my dark period. Your file was the thinnest of the bunch."

Violet sighed. "I'm deadly dull."

"You should do something to fix that," Scarlett teased before growing serious once more. "But getting back to the problem. Last night the thief stole all our files. Including one I pulled on Harper's mother." She paused, still unsure how much to share what she knew with Violet.

"If there's nothing much in the files, why would he risk getting caught stealing them?"

"He might have been fishing. I don't know if he went there looking for other files and just grabbed up whatever he could get or if he came specifically to take our family's files."

"But you said there was nothing of interest in them."

Again Scarlett hesitated. She knew she could trust Violet, but didn't want to anger Harper by spilling her secret. If it even was a secret. Maybe Harper knew. Maybe Grandfather knew. Maybe Scarlett and Violet were the only two in the dark.

But she didn't think that scenario was likely. Family meant too much to Henry Fontaine. It's why he'd given his illegitimate granddaughters the same shot at running Fontaine Hotels and Resorts as he'd given his legitimate one. Scarlett wasn't sure how he'd react if he found out Harper wasn't his granddaughter.

"Scarlett," Violet prompted, her tone tinged with alarm. "What aren't you telling me?"

"It's not about you. It's about Harper."

Violet laughed. "Harper? If anyone doesn't have skeletons in their closet it's her."

"It actually has to do with her mother. And what I discovered in the files has the potential of turning Harper's world upside down."

"If it's that bad," Violet said, dismay clouding her expression, "I don't want to ask what you unearthed."

Scarlett was relieved that Violet was letting her off the hook. The secret wasn't hers to share. If she told Harper, and if she in turn wanted Violet to know, that was different.

"Do I tell her?" Scarlett would love it if Violet told her what to do. "Would you want to know?"

Violet took a long time pondering Scarlett's questions. "I can't answer for Harper, but I don't think I'd want to know. Maybe it's awfully naive of me to think that anything that's been buried this long should stay hidden."

"Which is the way I was leaning before the files were stolen. But what happens if the guy figures out the same thing I did and the information gets out? She'll be blindsided. At least if I tell her, she can prepare."

"It's something she needs to prepare for?" Violet frowned. "In that case I don't think I can tell you what to do. On one hand, she deserves to know the truth."

So did other people. Like Grandfather. But Scarlett couldn't bear to be the one who damaged Harper's relationship with the man she looked up to and adored.

"On the other hand, the truth might ruin everything."

Logan entered his house and left his briefcase on the table in the foyer. Tugging at his tie, he strode into the kitchen to fetch a cold beer. He'd spent the better part of the afternoon in a meeting with a new client discussing a proposal that would be worth several million dollars over the next year or so.

Most of the new business Wolfe Security generated was handled by his sales staff. But every now and then a project came along where the client demanded to meet with Logan or Lucas. Considering this was the sort of deal that would strengthen their global-market position, Logan was willing to meet with the guy, no matter how much of a pain in the ass he was.

Beer in hand, he headed toward the master bedroom, intent on grabbing a shower and changing. He was heading back to Tiberius's storage unit next. Something about last night's theft had been nagging at him. Maybe another journey through the files would spark inspiration.

A tiny part of him recognized that visiting the storage unit was an excuse to avoid what he really wanted to do—spend time with Scarlett. All day long he'd caught himself reaching for the phone to call her. He'd known making love with her would aggravate his fascination with her. It was the reason that he'd resisted crossing that line for as long as he had.

He slowed as he neared Madison's room. "You're home early," he remarked, spying her facedown on her bed, feet kicking the air in slow sweeps.

She looked up from her reading, her gaze slow to focus

on him. "Scarlett gave me the night off. Said she needed to take care of something." Madison's smile grew sly. "Are you planning on staying out all night again?"

He ignored her question and asked one of his own. "What are you reading?"

"A script for a brand-new TV show. It's terrific. There's a part in here I'd be perfect for."

"Where did you get it?"

Madison's expression settled into worried lines. "I took it from Scarlett's office. I'll get it back before she even notices it's missing."

So Scarlett was reading scripts. And not just any scripts but ones featuring teenage girls. Surely she didn't think tempting the seventeen-year-old with juicy acting jobs that would never materialize was a good way to convince Madison to go to college? Did Scarlett think that once he'd given her his trust, she could go and do what she thought was right where Madison was concerned?

He prowled into the room. "Give me the script." His tone brooked no argument and he received none.

Madison sat up and handed him the bound pages. "I know I should have told her I wanted to read it, but she sounded so distracted when we spoke I didn't think she'd even notice."

To her credit, his niece sounded more apprehensive than argumentative. That was a change from the sullen teenager who'd appeared on his doorstep two weeks ago. Ten minutes ago he'd have been happy to give Scarlett credit for the transformation. That was before he found out she was looking at television projects.

"I'm sure if you'd asked her, she'd have let you read the script."

"You're right. I should have asked." Madison crossed

her legs and gave him her most solemn expression. "When you give it back to her tell her I'm sorry."

Giving Madison's repentant attitude a distracted nod, Logan continued toward his room. He finished showering and dressing in record time and was back on the road before his hair had a chance to dry. The script on the passenger seat beside him kept his irritation fueled. Scarlett had assured him she was done with Hollywood. So why was she bothering with a script?

Before leaving the house, he'd texted her and found out she was heading back to her office after meeting with Violet. He had twenty minutes to ponder what had passed between the sisters as he navigated the traffic between his house and the Strip.

The floor containing the executive offices at Fontaine Richesse was still active at seven o'clock. He nodded brusquely at the employees he passed as he strode the hall to Scarlett's large corner office. She was behind her desk, attention focused on the computer, when he entered. In the split second it took her to notice him, his heart bumped powerfully in his chest.

She was as beautiful in her gold silk blouse as she'd been last night wrapped in nothing but his arms. With her hair scraped back in a low ponytail and simple gold jewelry at her ears and throat, she looked every inch the successful executive. And nothing at all like the passionate temptress who'd unraveled his control.

"Logan." Her smile drew him across the room to her. "I didn't expect to see you tonight."

Instead of circling the desk and snatching her into his arms, he sat down in her guest chair and dropped the script onto the uncluttered surface between them. Her fingers slid off the keyboard and onto her lap.

She frowned. "Where'd you get that?"

"Madison had it."

"Madison?" Acting as if it was of little importance, Scarlett picked up the pages and dropped them into the trash. "She must have come by while I was meeting with Violet."

"Why do you have a script, Scarlett?"

She got up from her desk and circled around to lean against the front. "A producer friend of mine sent it to me."

"Let me guess, you know a teenager who would be perfect for his new TV show."

"What?" Her eyes went wide as his accusation sunk in. "No. Of course not. Is that what you think?"

"What else should I think?"

"That maybe I was offered a part. A good part. Something I would be perfect for." Her tone was insistent, defensive.

"I thought you were done with Hollywood."

She hesitated slightly before saying, "I am." But it was a telling pause.

What happened to all her protestations about how difficult her life as an actor had been? Was all of that merely a defense mechanism to keep disappointment at bay? When the opportunity came along to resume her acting career, would she jump at it?

"Of course I am," she insisted, her voice gaining conviction. "I have a life here in Las Vegas."

"But if this opportunity had come along five years ago and you had to choose, which life would you have picked?"

"That's not a fair question."

Her protest told him her answer was not to his liking. "You'd have chosen to stay in L.A."

"Probably. But only because acting was all I knew. Moving to Las Vegas and taking over the running of this hotel wasn't an easy decision for me to make. I had no experience. Frankly, I was terrified of making a mistake."

"Everyone makes mistakes."

"Yes, but do everyone's mistakes mean millions of dollars are at risk?" With a deep breath she clamped down on her escalating aggravation until her composure returned. "All this speculation is a waste of time. What I might have chosen to do five years ago has no bearing on what I do today."

Relief washed over him. She wasn't going to leave Las Vegas. Leave him. "I guess I jumped to the wrong conclusion."

She widened her eyes dramatically. "Was that an apology?"

"No." He pulled her onto his lap. "This is."

His kiss let her feel all his frustration and longing. The emotions she aroused troubled him. How could he mistrust her and still want her this much? Saying it was simple lust didn't ring true. She'd become his last thought at night and his first one in the morning. He was mesmerized by her beauty and intrigued by the layers she kept hidden.

"Feel like ordering room service in my suite?" she asked him once he'd let her come up for air.

"Maybe later. I want to check out the files in the storage unit."

"They're not there."

"Where are they?"

"I had them moved to a secure records storage unit this morning."

"I wish you'd told me that's what you were doing."

"Why? They're perfectly safe. Grady was eager to get to work and I feel better with them someplace secure."

"I'm not convinced keeping the files is a good idea."

"I can't part with them until someone I trust goes through everything. Plus, their historic value can't be measured until we know what's there."

"Wasn't last night proof of how dangerous they could be for you? Tiberius lived awfully well for a man whose casino was barely staying out of the red."

"What are you saying?"

"If it was a plot for a TV series, what would you deduce?"

"That Tiberius was blackmailing people?"

"That may have been what got him killed."

"Even if I had a clue what to look for, I'm not planning on blackmailing anyone."

"Maybe not—"

"Maybe not?" She interrupted in mock outrage. "Definitely not."

"Very well, then. Definitely not. But just because you and I know that doesn't mean Tiberius's victims know that."

Nonplussed, she stared at him for several seconds. "Then I guess the smartest thing for me to do is get with a lawyer and make certain that if anything happens to me, the files go public."

Her calm determination impressed the hell out of him. This was no scared female in need of rescue. She was a woman who survived by her wits as well as her beauty.

Logan tightened his hold around her waist. "Then I guess until you meet with an attorney, I should plan on sticking with you."

"Twenty-four/seven?"

"Whatever it takes."

# Eight

Scarlett had chosen to have Madison's birthday party at Fontaine Chic's poolside nightclub, Caprice. During the day, the pool offered a sexy Mediterranean beach-lounge vibe. At night when the well-dressed young crowd showed up, it became an extension of the club.

With all of Madison's Las Vegas friends too young to drink, Logan had voiced concerns that the eight teenagers would get into trouble, but Scarlett had met the kids and knew that even if they partied on a regular basis, they understood that abusing her trust would lead to all sorts of misfortune in their future.

Everything would go smoothly. It had to. She'd given Logan her word that Madison's party would be as safe as it was fun. Nothing could get in the way of that. It was the reason she was double-checking her arrangements prior to showtime. She wanted to make sure all the waitstaff knew the kids were underage and shouldn't be served alcohol no matter what sort of identification they produced.

After an afternoon at the pool, Scarlett had arranged for them to enjoy a suite at Fontaine Richesse. There would be fabulous food, a birthday cake at ten, and later the boys would be escorted home in a limo while the girls enjoyed a slumber party.

Madison had been over the moon with the arrangements, cementing Scarlett's status as the coolest boss ever. Logan had accused her of buying Madison's good favor, but his street cred had risen significantly when he'd agreed to Scarlett's plans.

Scarlett was standing at the entrance to the club when the first of Madison's guests arrived. Two girls and the boy Madison had been dating for the past couple of weeks. Trent was tall and lean with serious eyes. He had been captain of the basketball team in high school and third in his class. Under his influence, Madison had begun talking more and more about going to college in the fall.

"You all look like you're ready to have fun," she said, nodding to the doorman to let them through the velvet rope. "I booked you into cabana four."

"Is Madison here?" Trent asked.

"She's having lunch with her uncle," Scarlett answered. "I expect her any minute."

"She thinks you're the best to do all this for her birthday."

The teenager's earnest declaration made Scarlett's heart bump. "I'm happy to do it. You only turn eighteen once."

As her gaze followed Trent and his two companions across the pool deck, Scarlett thought about her own eighteenth birthday. She'd been doing some pretty hard partying in the year leading up to it. The crowd she ran with in Hollywood had been wealthy and wild, hitting clubs, doing whatever they felt like. She stood watching Madison's friends and tried to remember when she'd last known such innocuous delight.

"Don't worry, Scarlett," the bouncer told her, misinterpreting her melancholy as concern. Dave had biceps the size of full-grown trees and a nose that looked as if it had been broken a few times. "We'll keep an eye on the kids. Everyone knows that Madison is Logan's niece."

"Thanks, Dave." She touched his arm to show her appreciation. "I can't have anything go wrong today."

Four more kids showed up before the birthday girl made an appearance. Scarlett directed them to their friends and wondered what could be keeping Madison. Logan had to know his niece was super excited about her birthday party. Why would he delay her? Knowing Logan, he was probably lecturing Madison on all the things she wasn't supposed to do for the next twelve hours.

Scarlett unlocked her phone's screen, preparing to call Logan, when it began to ring. It was her assistant calling.

Sandy's voice was an octave higher than normal as she explained the reason for her call. "Chase Reynolds was here." Although the words were professional enough, Sandy sounded more like an infatuated teenager than her usual unflappable self.

Scarlett couldn't stop herself from smiling. The six-foot-three-inch action hero turned director could electrify the most jaded starlets in Hollywood. Sandy wouldn't have a chance. Then her assistant's words sank in.

"He *was* there? You mean he left? Where did he go?"

"Logan and Madison stopped by to find you and he left with them."

Her stomach clenched. "Was anyone else with Chase?

"An older man. Balding. Bobby something."

Chase must have really turned on the charm. This was not the efficient way Sandy normally functioned.

"Bobby McDermott." Scarlett didn't wait for Sandy to confirm. "Did Chase and Bobby say where they were heading?"

"To find you."

Several unladylike curses raced through Scarlett's mind. She should have known that dodging Bobby's calls was a bad idea, but she thought he'd realize she was serious about her disinterest in the project and move on. Sure, she was perfect for the part, but there were a dozen other actresses that would fit the bill just as well.

Anxiety rushed to fill the space where contentment had been only minutes earlier. Bobby and Chase couldn't have appeared at a worse time. In the past two weeks, she and Logan had begun to form a connection, but he still didn't fully trust her. If he thought she'd been lying about returning to acting, it might damage the tentative rapport growing between them.

"Thanks for the heads-up," she told Sandy before disconnecting the phone.

She imagined Bobby filling in Logan on the reason for his visit and the TV series they wanted her to do. Her muscles tensed as she contemplated how disappointed Logan would be in her. Of course he would assume the worst— that she'd lied when she'd told him she wasn't interested in the part.

She'd worked herself into quite a panic by the time Madison stepped off the elevator, her gaze glued on Chase Reynolds's handsome face. Despite her grim, chaotic emotions, Scarlett's amusement flared. Chase's good looks and charisma were a forceful thing. What made him completely irresistible, however, was that beneath the larger-than-life movie star lurked a genuinely nice guy.

Scarlett's focus shifted from the movie hero to the real-life hero and her mood plummeted. Logan looked like an advancing army intent on total annihilation. When he caught sight of her standing at the entrance to the club, she decided she'd seen attacking pit bulls that looked friendlier.

Tearing her gaze from Logan's stony expression, she greeted Bobby. "Hi. What are you doing here?" Twenty years of acting wasn't enough to keep the tension from her voice, but only Logan seemed to notice.

"Well, if Mohammed won't come to the mountain…" Bobby boomed, his eyes crinkling as he left the rest of the idiom hanging. "You look fabulous as always." He leaned in to kiss her cheek.

From the corner of her eye, Scarlett caught Logan's expression shift into a glower. She ignored the hollow in her stomach and pulled back to smile at Chase. "Hello, Chase. Nice to see you again."

Chase nodded, sweeping her into a very tight, very friendly hug. "Been a while. And Bobby's right, you look great."

"Vegas agrees with me." She meant the remark for Logan, but when her eyes met his, they were hard and flat. His disapproval wasn't a surprise, but her anxious reaction to it was. Feeling this vulnerable with a man was a miserable sensation, but if she raised her defenses she might push Logan away. And that would be so much worse. "I see you've met Logan Wolfe and his niece, Madison."

"Yes," Bobby said. "She's been telling us that it's her eighteenth birthday today and you've planned a fun-filled day for her and her friends."

"Yes, and they're all waiting for her in the club." Scarlett wasn't sure if Madison heard her because the birthday girl's attention remained fixed on Chase. His blinding white smile and the glint in his light brown eyes had mesmerized her. "You shouldn't keep them waiting."

"Oh, I'm sure they won't mind."

"But you're the guest of honor." Scarlett's speaking glance was wasted on Madison, but Chase noticed. "Logan, why don't you escort Madison to cabana four and make sure you're happy with all the arrangements."

She put a slight emphasis on the final word, hoping he'd understand her message. To appease Logan she'd agreed to let four of his security people—two men and two women—hang out with the party. To keep them unobtrusive, Logan had caved to them guarding in bathing suits. The kids would be kept under observation and never know it.

"But…" Madison looked as if she'd rather die than have her uncle show up at her party, but before she could protest, Chase spoke up.

"I'll come, too," the actor said. "I've heard that Caprice is a terrific club."

"It's fabulous," Madison agreed, catching him by the arm and turning him toward the pool.

While the teenager practically floated into the club between Logan and Chase, Bobby said, "Beautiful girl. She told me she's an actress."

Scarlett recognized the look in Bobby's eye. "It's not what her parents want for her."

"She seems pretty headstrong."

"You don't know the half of it."

Bobby laughed at her tone. "You know, she might work as our main character's daughter."

Seeing that the producer wasn't kidding, Scarlett grabbed his arm. "Oh, please don't put that idea in her head. I'm supposed to be spending the summer convincing her to go to college. If she heads off to Hollywood instead and her uncle thinks I had anything to do with it, he'll kill me."

Her vehemence made Bobby's eyebrows go up. "Well, if it's that important to you, of course I won't say a word."

"Thank you."

Her gaze shot across the pool deck to where the four teenage girls had clustered around Chase. As handsome and perfect as he was, her attention was drawn to where Logan stood, conversing with one of his employees. He possessed a charismatic pull as potent as the movie star's, but was too serious-minded to let it shine. Scarlett experienced a delicious thrill as he caught her watching him. He looked powerful and dangerous as his eyes promised her they were going to have a long and intense conversation.

"Looks like you have your hands full at the moment," Bobby said. "And I'm feeling lucky. Perhaps we should catch up over drinks later."

She shifted her attention to the producer and smiled in relief. "That would be great. I'll have my assistant get you and Chase set up in a suite." As she called Sandy, Scarlett spotted Logan and Chase heading her way. Whatever they were talking about wasn't improving Logan's mood.

He practically vibrated with annoyance as he stopped beside her. "Chase here tells me that you two are doing a TV series together."

"Ah…" Scarlett felt off balance, as if she'd been struck by a rogue wave. This was not the time or place for this conversation. "That's not exactly true."

"No?" Logan demanded, his hard voice low. "So what is exactly true?"

"I told Bobby no." She shot the producer an apologetic look.

"If that's true, then why are they here?"

"To talk her into changing her mind," Chase explained. "The part could have been written specifically for her and she knows it."

"Then maybe she should move back to Hollywood and take it." His congenial tone didn't match the tightness around his mouth.

Stung by Logan's negative assumption about her, Scarlett hastened to correct him. "I'm not going anywhere. My life is here. I love what I'm doing." Why wouldn't he give her the benefit of the doubt?

"But you're an actress," Bobby insisted. "And a damn good one."

"Will you all stop ganging up on me?" Scarlett took Bobby and Chase by the arms and turned them toward the door. "You two run along and win some money. I'll see you in a couple hours."

With those two taken care of for the moment, Scarlett turned to her next problem, but before she could defend herself against the recriminations in Logan's eyes, a pair of slim arms slipped around her neck in a gleeful chokehold.

"You are the best. I can't believe Chase Reynolds came to meet my friends. He's so amazing."

"That's Chase for you. Always ready to make new friends." Released from the exuberant hug, Scarlett turned to smile at Madison.

"I can't believe you two used to date."

Scarlett's gaze shot to Logan. He had his phone out and was texting someone. She could only pray he hadn't heard. "Yes, well. It was a long time ago. Now, I hope the rest of the day isn't a letdown. I don't have anything to top that."

"No worries. Everything is fabulous. I'm so glad Uncle Logan let me hang with you this summer." She winked at Logan.

Scarlett patted Madison's arm. "You can show your gratitude by going to college this fall."

Madison rolled her eyes, but her smile was bright as she blew Logan a flirty kiss and returned to her guests.

"I'll be back around five to escort you to Richesse," Scarlett called after her. Then she turned her attention back to Logan. "You can stop looking all annoyed with me. No matter how perfect the part is, I'm not taking it."

Logan hated to feel her slip away from him bit by bit, but he didn't want to invest his heart only to have it crushed when she went back to her life in L.A. "Are you sure that's a good idea? If those two came all this way to meet with you in person, they must really want to work with you. Perhaps you're making a mistake by turning them down."

"You seem pretty eager to get rid of me," Scarlett pointed out. "What's the matter, Logan? Are you afraid you'll get used to having me around?"

Her remark hit way too close to home, but Logan had spent enough time with her these past few days to recognize the uncertainty she was trying to hide. Glimpsing her vulnerability took the edge off his irritation.

He took her hand and began pulling her out of the club. "I'm already used to having you around," he told her, his voice rough and unhappy.

"Then why...?"

"What do you want me to tell you?" he demanded. "That I don't want you to go?"

"That would be nice."

She looked resolute and yet hopeful at the same time. Was she really that clueless about how strongly she moved him? After the past few evenings they'd spent together, how was that possible? Making love with her had turned him inside out. He wanted her with a fierceness he'd never known before.

"I can't tell you that."

He didn't want to care one way or another what she did with her life. What they were doing wasn't serious or life-changing. They were simply indulging in some good old-fashioned lust. So what if he couldn't stop thinking about her? Or that he missed her whenever she wasn't around? When she returned to L.A., he'd have no further need to make up reasons to visit Fontaine Richesse. He could stop acting like a smitten fool and recommit his attention to the business.

"Why not?"

"Because you need to make up your own mind about what you're going to do with your future." Even as he said the words he wished them back. Hadn't he already lost one woman because his pride had kept him from asking her to stay?

"Maybe I want a little input from you. I thought something was happening here. Am I wrong?"

When he didn't immediately respond, she tossed her head and strode off, not once looking back to see if he would follow. Which, of course, he did. His long strides brought him even with her in seconds.

"I'm sorry I can't give you what you need." After seeing the hurt that lanced through her eyes, he opted to explain himself further. "If you decide to stay here because of something you think is happening between us, what are your expectations for down the road?"

"I don't know." She narrowed her eyes and regarded him warily. "What are you trying to say?"

"We're very different. We argue all the time. Do you see this thing between us going anywhere?"

"Obviously you don't."

From the sharpness of her tone, he realized she wasn't thinking in terms of a few weeks or even a few months. It shifted his perception. But no matter what either of them wanted, the fact remained that their personalities had a knack for rubbing each other raw. How long before passion faded and all that was left between them was a long list of grievances?

He liked her too much to end up with animosity between them.

"Tell me about the part those Hollywood guys came out to discuss with you."

"I don't know why they're so determined to have me." If any other woman had uttered those words, she might have been fishing for a compliment, but Scarlett wasn't reticent about her talent or her beauty. "I can think of a dozen other actresses who would be just as good or better."

"Maybe they all turned the part down."

She bestowed a droll smile on him. "Amazingly enough, I'm the first person they've offered the part to."

Logan hadn't meant his remark the way she took it. "I didn't mean to imply that you were a last choice. Based on what you've been saying about being committed to Fontaine Richesse, I thought you wanted me to believe you'd left your career behind in Hollywood."

"I did leave it behind." She sighed. "Mostly."

It was her equivocating that renewed his frustration. "But it followed you here."

"Bobby is a hard man to say no to."

"I suppose it depends on how sincere you were." Why couldn't she just admit that the offer intrigued her?

"You can't seriously believe that I would give up my life here?" She scrutinized his expression. "My family's here. I have a career I love, and things…have gotten very exciting."

He gripped her arm and stopped her. "What sort of things?" He hadn't meant to sound so intense. But he needed to hear her admit how she felt about him.

Her lips parted, but no words emerged. Finally, she shrugged. "Tiberius's unsolved murder. His files. My attack."

All of which meant she was in danger. Maybe returning to Hollywood wasn't such a bad idea. "All good reasons for you to leave Las Vegas and take the part."

Scarlett shook her head, then regarded him. "Why is it so damn important to you that I take Bobby's offer?"

Because he needed to prepare himself if she was going to leave.

"You have a knack for finding trouble. I just want to know when my life is going to get back to normal."

Irritation with Logan burned in Scarlett's chest during the hours after they parted until she returned to collect Madison and her friends and bring them back to Fontaine Richesse. She tried not to let his willingness to be rid of her dent her ego, but his "support" of her career had leveled a crushing blow to her heart. How had she so misread the situation between them? Granted, it wasn't easy getting past his hard exterior to the caring, passionate man beneath. But in the past two weeks, she'd thought she was starting to make inroads.

He'd never be a tender romantic, but she'd eat that sort of guy up in two bites. Logan was difficult and fascinating. She could spend a lifetime with him and never get bored. The tail end of the impulsive thought snagged her full attention.

When had she starting thinking in terms of a lifetime with Logan? Her immediate reaction was to shy away from her heart's answer. She reminded herself that her first description of the man was that he was difficult. Did she really want to spend the rest of her life with such an intractable male?

The answer was yes if the man was Logan Wolfe.

He was the only man she'd never been able to manipulate. This meant that she had to be her genuine self around him or he'd call her on it. That was both liberating and terrifying. Letting him glimpse her faults and vulnerabilities meant at any moment he could use her weaknesses against her. Would he?

A breathy laugh puffed out of her. And she'd accused *him* of having trust issues. She was not much better. She could count on one hand all the people she trusted in the world. The first was her mother. The next two, her sisters, Harper and Violet. The fourth, she was on her way to meet for a drink. Scarlett contemplated her thumb. Did she count Logan among her allies?

"Hello, Bobby," she said, sitting down beside the producer. "Is Chase joining us?"

"No. He's on a winning streak at the craps table and didn't want to leave."

Scarlett smiled. "What about you? Any luck at the tables?"

"A little." He grinned at her. "Now, let's get down to business. I know you, Scarlett. You want this part."

"It's a fabulous opportunity."

"So come to L.A. and test for it."

Agreeing would set her foot on a path that might not lead back to Las Vegas. She shook her head. "I really appreciate what you're trying to do for me," she told the producer. "But I'm not interested."

"You're an actress, not a hotel manager."

He made it sound as if she was dealing drugs for a living. "I'm not turning you down because of my position with Fontaine Richesse," she explained. "I have a life here. A life I really love."

"What if we could shoot all your scenes in one day? You wouldn't have to move back to Hollywood. Just commute. You still own your house, don't you?"

She had a place on the beach in Malibu that she'd bought

shortly after turning eighteen. She'd told herself she'd kept the house because market values had dropped, but the truth was she loved the California coast and kept it as a getaway when she needed to escape the glitter and rush that was Vegas.

Or as a backup plan?

Was Logan right? Deep in her heart, was she thinking of Las Vegas as something to fill the time during the lull in her acting career? With the way her heart was skipping at the thought of going back to work in front of the camera, she had to consider if she'd been kidding herself all this time.

"It's been seven years since I've done more than a guest spot here and there. What if I'm terrible?"

"Not possible."

She covered Bobby's hand and gave it an affectionate squeeze. "No one was beating down my door five years ago," she reminded him. "There had to be a good reason for that."

"You were turning down the parts offered."

"Because I wanted to do something that called for me to do more than look pretty and act sexy."

"Here's your chance."

"No wonder you're the most successful producer in Hollywood."

"I know what I want."

"And you don't stop until you get it."

"Then you'll come do the test?"

If Logan had asked her to stay, would she be at all tempted by Bobby's faith in her? Scarlett sighed. She'd never let a man sway her decision about anything. Why was she doing so now?

"Let me talk it over with my sisters. I'll let you know before you leave tomorrow."

Bobby's smile broadened with triumph. "Perfect."

Maybe Logan had been right about the message she was sending the producer. She'd gone from a definite no to agreeing to consider a screen test.

"If you'll excuse me," Scarlett said, getting to her feet, "I have some party arrangements to check on. Sandy secured you an eight-thirty reservation at Le Taillevent this evening. Dinner's on me."

"As always you're the perfect host." Bobby rose to his feet and leaned forward to kiss her cheek. "Chase and I are leaving at one tomorrow. Can you join us for lunch before we go?"

"Why don't I come to your suite at eleven-thirty."

"I'll see you then."

After getting Madison and her friends settled into the hotel suite with pizza and a warning to keep the music at a reasonable volume, Scarlett organized a quick dinner with her sisters in her suite at Fontaine Richesse. As the three sat down to salads topped with salmon and glasses of white wine, Scarlett quickly broached what was on her mind.

"I've had an offer to do a television series," she said, sipping her wine.

As usual, Harper was the first to react. "I thought you were done with acting."

"I was." Scarlett heard the uncertainty in her tone and qualified her response. "I mean, I thought I was."

"Is it an interesting part?" Violet quizzed.

"The best I've ever been offered."

"A lead?" Harper was the sort who set her eyes on the top prize and wouldn't consider anything less worth her time.

"No. It's a small supporting role, but the character is complex and interesting." Scarlett looked at each of her sisters. "Five years ago, even two years ago, I wouldn't have hesitated to race back to L.A. and take the part."

"But now?" Violet prompted. "Something's changed?"

"I really feel as if I've hit my stride with the hotel. Then there are you guys. I love being your sister and don't want to live so far away from you."

"That's awfully sweet of you to say." Harper's lips curved in a dry smile. "But are you forgetting that we're your chief competition in our grandfather's contest?"

Scarlett laughed at Harper's question, despite her lingering uneasiness over her decision to conceal what she knew about her sister's true parentage. "You don't seriously think I have a shot at running Fontaine Hotels and Resorts, because I'm convinced I don't."

"You don't know that," Violet insisted, always the peacemaker. "Fontaine Richesse has done really well under your management. Grandfather could choose you."

"I don't have the experience or the education required to run the company." Scarlett pointed her fork first at Harper, then at Violet. "You two are the only ones in the running. I'm just happy to have been given the chance to be considered."

"Have you told Logan that you're thinking about heading back to L.A.?" Violet asked.

"Logan?" Harper interjected before Scarlett could answer. "Why would she tell him?"

"Because they've been seeing each other," Violet said, her tone exasperated. "Don't you notice anything that happens outside your hotel?"

"Not in the past three weeks." She turned to Scarlett. "How serious is it?"

Scarlett lifted her hand to bat away the question, but the concern laced with curiosity in her sisters' eyes was a powerful thing. "It could be anything from casual to involved. I can't really tell. He's pretty cagey about his emotions."

"Cagey?" Harper echoed, her tone doubtful. "He's positively Alcatraz. I've gotta say, I didn't see that coming. You two are like oil and water."

"More like gasoline and matches," Violet put in. "All that animosity between you had to be hiding a raging passion."

Scarlett didn't comment on her sister's observation, but couldn't prevent heat from rising in her cheeks. As an actress she could control her body language and facial expressions, but stopping a blush was something she'd never mastered.

"Raging passion?" Harper echoed, her eyes widening. "What exactly have I been missing?"

"A lot." Violet looked smug. "How many nights has he stayed at your place in the past two weeks?"

"Not one." He liked to be home when Madison got up in the morning.

"Then how many nights has he gone home in the wee hours of the morning?"

"Several." Scarlett couldn't believe how giddy she felt at the admission.

"Then it's serious?" Harper asked.

"He's encouraging me to head back to L.A. and take the part. That tells me it's pretty casual."

"But hot," Violet piped up.

Both Harper and Scarlett ignored her.

"Maybe he knows how important acting is to you and wants you to be happy," Harper suggested with a pragmatic nod.

"But I told him I was done with acting."

"But you're telling us that you're not."

"I really thought I was. It's been a year since I've been

offered a guest spot. And that's been fine. I've been completely content here. I put L.A. and acting behind me." Scarlett sorted through her conflicting emotions. "I've already turned down Bobby three times, but he won't take no for an answer and after Logan told me to go, I'm wondering why I'm hesitating."

"Why *are* you hesitating?" Harper asked.

"You're going to think I'm an idiot."

Violet said, "I promise we won't."

"Logan is so against my past acting career and I didn't want to do anything to jeopardize our relationship. But today he was behaving like there's nothing going on with us. I'm starting to think I made up our connection because I'm crazy about him." Admitting her deep feelings wasn't something that came easily to Scarlett, but time spent with her sisters had eroded the walls she kept up to guard against disappointment and hurt.

"You are?" Violet looked surprised. "How crazy?"

"The kind that's going to end up with my heart broken." Being able to share her concerns with Harper and Violet gave Scarlett a sense of relief. "Maybe I should go back to L.A. and take up my career again."

"We'd miss you," Violet told her.

"We would."

Scarlett's eyes burned. "Thanks."

"I'll bet Logan would miss you, too," Violet said, her hazel eyes sparkling. "Maybe he's pushing you away because he's afraid it will hurt too much to lose you."

That sounded sweet to Scarlett's ears, but she wasn't susceptible to romance the way Violet was. In fact, until Logan came along, she'd interacted with men with an eye toward what they could do for her.

"Logan Wolfe isn't afraid of anything," Scarlett declared. "Least of all losing me."

"Everyone's afraid of something," Harper said in an un-usual display of insight. "You'll just have to figure out if he's more afraid of keeping you around or letting you go."

# Nine

Logan paced his living room, aware that he resembled a grumpy, caged bear. He squinted against the sunlight streaming in his large picture window, but Scarlett's flashy red convertible was not streaking up his driveway. For the tenth time in half an hour he glanced at his watch. Not surprisingly, the hands hadn't crept forward more than a couple minutes. It was 12:23 p.m. and Madison should have been home from her birthday party almost two hours ago.

If something happened to her…

A car was moving through the vegetation that lined the driveway, but it wasn't Scarlett's. As the vehicle drew closer, Logan spied his niece in the passenger seat and recognized Scarlett's assistant as the driver. Annoyed by the change in plans, Logan strode through the front door and went to meet the car.

"Hey, Uncle Logan." Madison exited the car, her overnight bag slung over her shoulder, and waved at the driver.

She stretched and yawned with dramatic flair as she neared him. "What a birthday party. That was the most fun I've ever had." Lifting up on tiptoe, she kissed his cheek. "Thanks again for letting Scarlett plan the party."

"Where is she? She was supposed to drive you home."

His sharp tone caused Madison's eyes to widen. "She had a meeting with Bobby and Chase, so she had Sandy bring me home. You can't disapprove of Sandy, Uncle Logan. She's thirty-five, never had a ticket. She drove the speed limit the whole way here."

Ignoring Madison's sass, Logan focused on what was really bothering him.

"So it's Bobby and Chase, now, is it?" he demanded, his temper getting the better of him. "When did you get so cozy with them?"

He knew better than to take his frustration out on his niece. It was Scarlett who'd stirred up his ire. Scarlett who was hell-bent on returning to L.A. and her acting career.

Or maybe he was mad at himself for encouraging her to do so.

"I'm not cozy with them," Madison retorted. "They were just being nice. Bobby gave me his card and Chase told me to look him up when I get to L.A."

Logan's focus sharpened. "What do you mean, when you get to L.A.? You're heading to college this fall."

Madison tossed her hair in a perfect imitation of Scarlett at her most exasperating. In fact, now that he thought about it, Madison had adopted several mannerisms from the actress. How had he not noticed the metamorphosis before this? His niece admired everything about Scarlett, why wouldn't she think it was a good idea to behave like her?

"I know my parents sent me here so you could work on me about college, and heaven knows that's a drum Scarlett has beaten to death, but I really think my path lies in

Hollywood." She rested her hand on her hip and tilted her chin. "And I'm eighteen now. I can do whatever I want."

Logan ground his teeth and regarded Madison in silence. This wasn't the tune she'd been singing yesterday morning. She'd been debating two of the schools she'd gotten into, trying to decide which way to go.

"You might be eighteen, but you've never been on your own without your parents' money before."

"I'll get a job waiting tables or something and support myself until I get an acting job."

Logan was beset by visions of his niece all alone and at the mercy of a string of people with bad intentions who would use Madison up and spit her out. "Do you really think it will be that easy?" How had weeks of good advice been erased in one short night? "And where are you going to live?"

"I can stay with Scarlett."

Icy fingers danced up Logan's spine. So Scarlett had decided to return to L.A., after all. And why not? Hadn't he told her to go?

"She's definitely moving back to L.A.?" he asked, trying to keep his voice neutral.

Madison looked surprised that he even had to ask. "Of course. Why would she turn down a part that will kick-start her career once more?"

The thought of losing her swung a wrecking ball at his gut. He'd been a fool to let her think he would be unaffected by her departure. Had he really thought this was a good time to test her? To see if she meant all her passionate kisses and romantic gestures? Sheer stubbornness had made him complacent that she'd choose Las Vegas and him over her acting career and stardom.

"Did she invite you to stay with her?"

"Not in so many words, but I know she will do whatever she can to help me get started."

Hadn't she already done enough? Logan fished his car keys out of his pocket. He and Scarlett needed to have a face-to-face chat.

"We'll talk more about this when I get back."

"Where are you going?" She sounded less like a confident woman and more like a teenager who was worried she'd pushed her luck too far.

"To talk with Scarlett."

"What are you going to say?"

"That you are not going to L.A., so she can forget about having you as a roommate."

"It won't do any good. She was thrilled that Bobby was willing to help me."

Two weeks ago Logan might have believed Madison's claim. Since then, Scarlett had stuck to his wishes and encouraged the teenager to finish college before she made any career choices. He also knew just how headstrong Madison could be. She'd proven that when she'd run off to L.A. on her own last spring.

"Why don't you give your parents a call and tell them how the party went yesterday. I'm sure they're eager to hear how you spent your birthday."

He was heading his Escalade down the driveway when his phone rang. He cued the car's Bluetooth. "Wolfe."

"Boss, it's Evan. You wanted me to let you know when the Schaefer assessment was done. Jeb and I finished half an hour ago. The report is on your desk."

"Thanks."

Preoccupied with the troublesome women in his life, he'd forgotten all about the multimillion-dollar proposal they were working on to overhaul Schaefer Industries's security system. The deadline for the bid was four this afternoon. He needed to look over the final numbers and make sure there were no holes in the strategy they'd created. Scarlett would have to wait.

The big closet full of costumes wasn't having its usual soothing effect on Scarlett. She grazed her fingertips along sequined sleeves and plucked at organza skirts but couldn't summon up the charisma to wear Marilyn Monroe's white dress from *The Seven Year Itch* or the slinky green number Cyd Charisse wore to dance with Gene Kelly in *Singin' in the Rain*. Her heart was too heavy to play her namesake, Scarlett O'Hara, and she'd never be able to pull off Cleopatra's sexy strength.

Her confidence had been dipping lower and lower ever since she'd told Bobby her decision about the television series. Logic told her she'd chosen correctly, but she couldn't shake the worry that she'd irrevocably closed the door because she was afraid of putting herself out there and being rejected.

She came across Holly Golightly's long black dress from the opening scene of *Breakfast at Tiffany's,* pulled it off the rack and held it against herself. Perfect. Holly's mixture of innocence and street savvy had always struck a chord in Scarlett. Many days she felt that way. Tough on the outside because acting was a rough business to be in. Fragile as dandelion fluff on the inside. Some weeks she'd go for a dozen auditions and not have a single callback. It had been hard on her, a change from the days when she'd basked in the studio's love and appreciation.

Running Fontaine Richesse had brought her defenses and her longing into balance. She'd gained confidence in her abilities and no longer faced daily rejection. Dropping her guard had taken a while, but eventually she'd stopped expecting to hear what she was doing wrong. She'd begun to thrive.

Scarlett put on the iconic black dress, zipped it up and fastened on a collar of pearls. She regarded her reflection in the mirror. This costume was a head turner. With the sixties-style wig, black gloves and long cigarette holder, she bore an uncanny resemblance to Audrey Hepburn. And becoming Holly Golightly gave her a much-needed break from her current worries.

It's what she loved about acting. Becoming another person was like taking a vacation without going anywhere. For twelve or fourteen hours at a time she was transported to a simple house in the suburbs where her parents laughed at misunderstandings about fixing dinner and her siblings got into trouble at school. Simple complications that resolved themselves in twenty-two minutes. Where lessons were learned and everyone hugged and smiled in the end.

The pleasure such memories gave Scarlett reaffirmed that she was an actress at heart. It was something that would always come between her and Logan. He preferred everything straightforward and realistic. She was pretty sure he wasn't the sort of man who wanted his woman to dress up like a naughty schoolgirl, a cheerleader or even Princess Leia. Which was too bad because she had a copy of Leia's slave girl costume tucked away in her closet.

As she tugged on the elbow-high black gloves, she heard a knock on her door. Her heart jumped into her throat as she raced across the living room. More cautious after her attack, she checked the peephole and saw Logan standing in the hall. They hadn't spoken all day. She'd been both hoping and dreading that he'd call. She was terrified to tell him about her decision. Although he'd encouraged her to take the part, it was such an about-face from his earlier stance on her career, she didn't understand his motives.

Breath uneven, she threw open the door, uncertain about what to expect. His tight mouth and fierce gaze stopped her forward momentum. A muscle jumped in his jaw as he stepped into her suite, compelling her to shift to one side or be trampled.

"Hello, Logan."

He strode past her without responding and began pacing in the middle of the room.

"Don't go."

His brusque tone matched the tension vibrating off him. She was used to his demanding ways, actually enjoyed surrendering to his desires. Not that she would ever admit it. Ninety-nine percent of the time she preferred being in complete control. It was a throwback to her days in Hollywood when she'd had very little power. But she had learned she could trust Logan and it was nice to hand over the reins once in a while.

"Sure. It won't matter if I don't make an appearance in the casino tonight." Her body tightened with hunger as she moved toward him. "What did you have in mind?"

He spun to face her. "I don't mean tonight. I mean at all."

Scarlett stretched out her arm and set her palm against his shoulder, treating him like a skittish dog, trying to gentle his mood with her touch. "Logan, I'm in charge of this hotel. I don't see how I can stay away from my own casino."

His arm snaked around her waist and brought her tight against his body. "Not the casino, you simple-minded darling. Don't go to Los Angeles."

"But you said—" She broke off when he stroked his hand up the side of her neck and wrapped his fingers around the back of her head.

"I know what I said." He leaned down and seized her mouth with his, short-circuiting her brain.

The kiss was so like him. Commanding, skillful, hungry. He claimed her breath, stole her willpower and insisted on her complete surrender. Whether he'd admit it or not, he found her strength attractive. What if her weakness disgusted him? One way or another, she needed him to see the real her. Only by letting him glimpse her fear of rejection could she be free.

Terror and joy washed over her as she unraveled in his arms. Immediately, the kiss softened. Passion became play as his tongue and teeth toyed with and tantalized her.

How had she ever dreamed she could leave him? Only with Logan did she feel this alive and complete. She broke off the kiss and arched her back as his lips trailed fire down her neck. Gasping as his teeth nipped at her throat, she struggled to clear her thoughts from the drugging fog of desire.

"I'm not going to take the part," she murmured, kissing his temple and the bold stroke of his dark eyebrow. "I'm not going to L.A."

He straightened and peered into her eyes. "Madison said you were going to accept the role."

"I never told her that." If the teenager's misunderstanding had caused Logan to admit how he truly felt, Scarlett would make certain she would do something extra nice for the girl. Maybe a day at the spa. "I don't know where she got such an idea."

"She said you were having breakfast with that producer fellow."

"I did. I told Bobby once and for all that I wasn't going to take the part."

"But you wanted to." Logan took her left hand and began peeling the black glove down her arm.

The drag of the fabric against her sensitized skin made Scarlett shiver. "For seventeen years my identity was caught up in being an actress."

He hooked his finger beneath her pearl necklace and stroked her feverish skin. "I don't see where anything has changed in that respect."

She smiled as Logan set to work on the other glove. Being undressed by him was always such a treat. Occasionally their hunger for each other grew too feverish for preliminaries, but most of the time he took such pleasure in every aspect of making love, from removing her clothes to cuddling with her in the aftermath of passion.

"I think I'll always be an actress in my heart," she assured him. "But that's no longer all I am. Managing this hotel has shown me that I'm also a darned good businesswoman." She tunneled her now-naked fingers into his hair and pulled his head toward her. "I'm glad you didn't want me to go, because I didn't want to leave you."

This time when they kissed, he let her lead. She understood why as her dress's zipper yielded beneath his strong fingers. He stroked the material off her shoulders and left her standing before him in her pearls, a strapless black bra and panties and black pumps. His gaze burned across her skin as he took in the picture she made.

Divesting herself of the necklace and casting aside her wig, Scarlett stripped away the final trappings of Holly Golightly. The character was a woman with many lovers, but no burning love. She was a wild thing who craved freedom even as, deep in her heart, she longed for a place to belong.

Scarlett had no such conflicts. She knew exactly what she wanted, just as she knew where she belonged. In Logan's arms. Pretending to be someone else, even for a while, couldn't compare to the reality of being herself, in love with him. Her throat contracted as she realized why she'd turned down the part. It wasn't just because she loved her new life as the manager of Fontaine Richesse. It was because she loved Logan Wolfe and all the heartache and joys that went along with being the woman in his life.

Lifting onto her tiptoes, she wrapped her arms around his neck and kissed him firmly on the mouth. "Take me to bed, you big bad hunk."

"Your wish is my command."

Logan scooped Scarlett into his arms and headed for her bedroom, glad he'd followed his instincts and sought her out tonight. Those six hours between learning she'd decided to return to L.A. and showing up at her suite had been hell and he had no interest in reliving them anytime soon. His unhappiness at her leaving had forced him to assess just how reluctant he was to be without her.

How far would he have gone if she'd been determined to leave Las Vegas? Once upon a time he'd let Elle go and had never really stopped regretting it. What was happening between him and Scarlett claimed neither the duration nor the depth of what he'd shared with his ex-fiancée, but he felt as invested as if they'd been together for years.

Laying Scarlett on her bed, he began unfastening his shirt buttons. She made no attempt to remove her bra or panties, knowing he preferred to strip her bare himself. All she did was shake her hair free of the pins that held it in place and kick off her shoes.

She lifted herself onto one elbow and twirled a lock of her hair as she watched him shuck off his shirt and send his pants to the floor. She gave him a sultry, heavy-lidded look as she waited for him to join her.

He trailed his fingertips up her thigh and felt her shudder as his thumb whisked along the edge of her panties. With a half smile, he used his hands to memorize each rise and dip of her body. No matter how many times he touched her, he found something new to fascinate him. With her full breasts and hourglass shape, she was built for seduction, but as he'd discovered the first time he'd made love with her, she had a romantic's soul.

Taking her hand, he kissed the inside of her wrist, lips lingering over her madly beating pulse. He'd cataloged about a hundred ultrasensitive areas on her body and enjoyed revisiting them each time they made love. The inside of her elbow was mildly ticklish and she loved being lightly caressed on her arms. He did so now and was rewarded when she uttered a little hum of delight, her version of a purr.

It had taken her a bit to realize he wasn't going to rush the sex between them. Even when they were both too caught up in their passion to enjoy extended foreplay, he made certain to arouse her with words as well as hands and mouth.

He leaned forward to kiss her mouth, pressing her back against the pillows. She melted against him, soft curves yielding to all his hard planes. They kissed long and slow, enjoying the blending of their breath, the feint and retreat of tongues. Logan slipped his hands beneath her and rolled them a half turn so she sat astride him.

She lifted her hair off her shoulders, arching her back and tilting her breasts toward the ceiling. Her movements were measured and graceful like a cat indulging in a languid stretch after rising. The flow of muscle beneath her soft skin mesmerized him. He ran his hands over her rib cage, riding their waves upward until he reached the lower curve of her breasts. Through half-closed eyes she watched him cup her breasts through the black lace and gently massage.

Reaching behind her, she popped the bra clasp and the fabric sagged into his hands. He tossed it aside and traced the shape of her breasts with his fingertips. He circled the tight nipples, noticing that she rocked her hips in time with his caresses, easing the ache he inflicted on her.

His erection bobbed with her movements, the sensitive head scraping against her lace-covered backside and aggravating his already ravenous hunger. As much as he yearned to seat himself inside her, the pleasure he received from watching her desire build made the wait worthwhile.

Noticing his eyes upon her, Scarlett shook her head, her hair cascading about her shoulders in riotous waves. Some of it fell forward over her face and she peeked at him from between the strands, her eyes beckoning. Setting her hand on his chest, she bent forward and planted a lusty, open-mouthed kiss on him, showing her delight in the moment with a deep thrust of her tongue.

Logan filled his hands with her firm backside.

"Let's get these off you, shall we?"

"Please do."

Working together, they slid her panties down her thighs. As he tossed them aside, she produced a condom and used her teeth to tear open the package. Logan braced for the wonderful pain of what would come next and locked his jaw as she fitted the protection over the head of his erection, and with a thoroughness that was both a torment and a treat, rolled it down his shaft. A groan ripped from his throat as she finished, but she gave him no chance to recover before settling herself onto him.

The shock of being encased in so much heat so suddenly made his hips buck. She rode his movement with a faraway smile and a rotation of her pelvis.

"Geez, Scarlett," he muttered, wiping sweat from his brow. "Warn a guy."

"What's the fun in that?"

And fun is what she was having. Letting her do whatever she wanted with him was almost as entertaining as making her squirm. Half his delight came from watching her explore his chest and abs while maintaining that delightful rhythm with her hips. She was a living, breathing goddess and Logan couldn't take his eyes off her.

But the chemistry between them had a mind of its own and soon they were both swept into a frenzy of movement where each surge pushed them closer to the edge. Wanting to watch her come, Logan slipped his hands between them and touched the button of nerves that would send her spinning into the abyss. Her eyes shot wide, signaling the beginning of her orgasm. She clenched him tight, increasing the friction, and he pitched into the black, spinning in a vortex of pleasure so intense it hurt.

With a whoosh of air from her lungs, she collapsed forward and buried her face in his neck. Logan didn't have enough breath to voice his appreciation of what had just happened, so he settled for a firm hug and a clumsy kiss on her shoulder.

His heart rate took a long time returning to normal. The way she affected him, Logan wasn't surprised. Since that first kiss in the elevator, she'd shattered his serenity and caused him to reevaluate what made him happy. For a long time he'd resisted accepting how much he needed her. Today, he stopped fighting.

And now she was all his.

"I'm going to make damn sure you don't regret turning down the part," he told her, gliding his fingertips along her soft skin.

She laughed breathlessly. "I like the sound of that. Can we start now?"

He snagged her questing fingers and returned them to his chest. "I can't stay. I promised Madison that when I got back we'd talk about her moving to L.A."

"What?" Scarlett made the leap from languid to outraged in an eye blink. She pushed herself up so she could meet his gaze. "But yesterday she was talking about college."

Logan approved of her irritation. It matched his own. "Apparently that changed after she met your producer friend and Chase Reynolds."

Her face shuttered. "Bobby is a man who makes things happen and Chase is larger than life. I can see how they could've reawakened her dreams of going to L.A., but she and I talked about how important college was to your family. She agreed to get her degree and afterward, if she was still determined to be an actress, to then go to L.A."

"Apparently Bobby gave her his card and told her to look him up." Logan recalled the rest of what his niece had said. "She believed since you were returning to your acting career that you would offer her a place to stay."

A pained expression twisted Scarlett's features. "I'm sorry she got the wrong impression of what I intended to do. As for Bobby, I know he really liked her," she admitted in a low voice. "Even told me he might have a part for her in an upcoming TV series. I told him not to mention anything about it to her. I guess I should have been clearer and told him not to give her any encouragement at all."

"That might have been a good idea."

Scarlett tried to stay calm as she was caught in the riptide of Logan's growing annoyance. "I told him she was going to college this fall. I'm sure he didn't expect her to change her plans because he told her to look him up."

"There must have been more to it."

"I'll call her tomorrow and get her back on the path to college."

"I'd really appreciate that."

"My pleasure.

"Maybe she's just impatient to start living her dream," Scarlett suggested. "I certainly don't blame the girl for going after what she wants."

Placing her palm on Logan's chest, she set her chin on

her hand and scrutinized him. What was it about this often difficult, sometimes surprising and always sexy man that turned her insides into mush? They were at odds as much as they were in accord, but whether they were arguing or making love, he always made her feel as if being with her was exactly where he wanted to be.

And for that matter, what did he find appealing about her? He was scornful of her lack of a college education. Disparaging about her former occupation. Critical of her wardrobe, her abilities as a businesswoman and the way she used her sexuality to her advantage.

Granted, the chemistry between them was off the charts, but she was pretty sure she wasn't just a conquest. No, there was something more between them than fantastic sex, but she had no idea what.

"I'll tell you what," she said into the silence. "I'll talk to her tomorrow and get her back on the college track. Will that make you happy?"

"Are you sure you can do that?"

She had absolutely no clue. "Haven't I been doing a great job so far?" She acknowledged his skepticism with a wry smile. "Up until yesterday, I mean?"

"You have."

"Grudging praise from Logan Wolfe? I'm thrilled."

With a humph, he deposited a brief kiss on her mouth and began rolling toward the side of the bed where he'd left his clothes.

"Do you have to go?" Scarlett flopped onto her stomach and kicked her legs slowly in the air. As if drawn by a force too powerful to resist, his gaze swept over her disheveled hair and toured her naked backside. She knew exactly how appetizing she looked lying there and thrust out her lower lip in a provocative pout. "If you stay the night I'll make it worth your while."

Logan paused with his boxers in one hand, his shirt in the other. "How?"

"Let's see." She tapped her chin with a finger. "I can cook you breakfast."

"You mean order room service."

"I'll listen with interest as you tell me all about your work."

"You'd be snoring in five minutes."

"I don't snore." She pursed her lips and frowned as if in deep thought. "There's always morning sex." At last she'd found something to pique his interest. "I'm very energetic after a good night's sleep."

He dropped his clothes and rolled her onto her back. "How are you after no sleep at all?"

"Try me," she dared, wrapping her arms around his neck to pull him down for a kiss. "And find out."

# Ten

"See," Scarlett murmured, sounding sleepy and smug. "I told you morning sex was worth sticking around for."

Logan slipped a hand along her delicate spine as she set her cheek against his heaving chest. He soothed a strand of dark hair off her damp forehead and deposited a kiss just above her brow.

"I never doubted you for a second." Logan rolled her onto her back and kissed her slow and long.

The sky visible through Scarlett's bedroom window was a bright blue. Not wishing to set a bad example for Madison, he'd never stayed the whole night with Scarlett. She'd said she understood his reasons.

But last night he'd let her see how much she meant to him, and sharing his emotions with her had increased the intimacy between them. Leaving had been impossible, so he'd called the guy keeping an eye on Madison and told him to stay until morning.

Tangled in sheets and warm, naked woman, he pushed all thought to the back of his mind and concentrated on the contour of her lips, the way she moaned when he licked at her nipples and the unsteady beat of her heart as he nibbled on her earlobe.

"Last night was amazing." She burrowed her face into his neck so he couldn't see her expression. "I'm really glad you came by."

"I'm glad you decided to stay in Las Vegas."

"You were pretty sure I needed to go."

"I wanted my life to get back to normal."

She put her hand on his chest and pushed him back so she could look into his eyes. "Has that changed?"

"No." He flopped onto his back beside her and set his hands behind his head. Staring at the ceiling, he debated how much to tell her. "But I'm not sure I recognize what's normal anymore."

She rolled onto her side and rested her head on her palm. "What does that mean?"

"You've bothered me from the first moment we met." The words came out of him slowly. "Whenever we're in the same room it seems as if my senses sharpen. I can discern your voice amongst a dozen others. Your perfume seems to get on my clothes and infiltrate my lungs. And when I close my eyes it's your face, your eyes, your body I see." From her wide eyes and open mouth, he gathered his romantic blathering had surprised her. Logan let a smile creep over his lips. "In short, I've been obsessed with you for five years."

"Were you one of those little boys that shoved and shouted at the girl he liked because he didn't want to be teased for liking her?"

"I don't remember." He did recall in junior high that he'd been a lot more comfortable with computers than the girls in his class. While his buddies were serial-dating, he'd been modifying motherboards and hacking into the school's database. "Lucas was the one who excelled with the opposite sex ever since he was six years old. Always dating someone. Most of the relationships didn't last more than a couple of months before he was on to someone new."

"You are never going to get me to believe that you were a monk."

"Not a monk. I had a steady girlfriend from the time I turned fourteen. We dated all through high school and college."

"Fourteen?" She gave him a wry grin. "What happened after school?"

This was the part he didn't like talking about. After ten years, it still stung. "She chose her career over me and moved to London."

"Why didn't you go with her?"

Because he'd been too stubborn and arrogant to realize he was losing the best thing that had ever happened to him. "My life was here. I'd started a computer security company and I wasn't about to give it all up."

"Then it couldn't have been that serious."

Resentment burned at her easy dismissal of what had been the most important relationship of his life. "We'd been dating almost nine years. Been engaged for three."

"But neither one of you had pulled the trigger. Maybe it was more about how comfortable and easy it was than that you were in love."

His temper continued to heat. She was the furthest thing from an expert on how he felt.

"You weren't there." He'd devoted years to loving Elle. Giving up a future with her hadn't been easy. "You can't possibly know how it was between us."

"Of course not," she soothed. "I'm simply pointing out

that if she'd been your everything you'd have figured out a way to stay together."

It cut like glass that he considered the merits of her argument for even a second. He and Elle had been devoted to each other for nine years, and he had let her go without much of a fight. Just like he'd been ready to let Scarlett move to L.A. Only this time, he'd come to his senses and asked her to stay. He hadn't done the same with Elle. She'd been determined to go, asked him to join her, but he'd never requested she turn down the job offer. Had she been waiting for him to?

"From your expression, I'm going to guess something new has crossed your mind," Scarlett said. "Care to tell me what?"

"You might be right. Maybe what kept us together all through school was that we were traveling the same path."

"Sometimes that's the only thing that does keep people together. Giving up your dream so another can live theirs isn't a sacrifice many are willing to make."

"When I came in tonight you were dressed up. No matter how dedicated you are to managing this hotel and competing against your sisters to run Fontaine Hotels and Resorts, you are at heart an actress." He noted the way her lashes flickered at his statement. "Are you sacrificing what you truly want to stay here?"

"I made a choice between two heart's desires," she said, her smile cryptic. "And I'm never going to second-guess myself about it." With a languid stretch she swung her feet to the floor and stood. "I'm going to grab a shower. Want to join me?"

After an early lunch in her suite, Logan headed to Wolfe Security, leaving Scarlett to wander downstairs to her office in a happy daze. She sat down behind her desk and stared out over the Las Vegas skyline, hoping no big emergencies came up while she was in this state of bliss because she couldn't count on her problem-solving abilities.

Her cell phone rang at a little after two o'clock, rousing her out of a pleasant memory of the night before. It was Grady.

"Scarlett, I think you are going to want to come down here and see what I found in Tiberius's files."

After the theft of documents in her suite, they'd agreed nothing was to leave the secure-documents facility.

"Can you tell me what it is?"

"I'd rather not. You will want to see it for yourself."

Disturbed by Grady's caginess, Scarlett grabbed her car keys and headed for the door. "I'm going to MyVault Storage," she told Sandy as she left. "I'll be back by four for the senior staff meeting."

Through most of the half-hour drive she wondered what Grady might have found. The fact that he'd been reluctant to share the information over the phone had been odd. What, was he thinking that someone could be listening in? For an instant all she could see was the man in the ski mask. How easy it would have been to plant listening devices in her suite while she was unconscious. Almost as soon as the thought occurred, she brushed it away. Logan's paranoia was beginning to rub off on her.

She used her key card and entered the facility. The security guard in the lobby nodded in recognition as she signed in. Cameras watched her from three directions. The security had seemed a little much when she'd first visited the place, but right now she was glad she'd listened to her gut.

Halfway down a long corridor, she stopped in front of a door marked 23. Again she used her key card to gain access. Grady spun around as she entered. She noted his pale complexion and startled gaze and decided he needed to spend a little less time here.

"Have you eaten lunch?" She held up a bag of Chinese food and a six-pack of Diet Mountain Dew, his favorite.

"No. I was going to go grab something before I found this." He nudged a file toward her and accepted the bag of takeout.

What he showed her was an old photo of a group of teenagers. One of them looked familiar, but she couldn't place why.

"This is a photo of someone named George Barnes and his buddies." Grady turned the photo over and showed her the names jotted down on the back. "There's an old police report from 1969 that mentions George Barnes as well as a few other guys in this photo in connection with some neighborhood burglaries, but nothing was ever solid enough to arrest any of them."

"So Barnes was a bad kid." Despite her confusion, Scarlett felt a jolt of excitement at the old documents and what they meant to Grady.

"In another file, I found this newspaper clipping about an accidental drowning during a storm. A local boy by the name of George Barnes had been killed. An eighteen-year-old kid from California had tried to save him. A wealthy, orphaned kid by the name of Preston Rhodes."

"Preston Rhodes?" Scarlett looked from the article to the photo. "As in Tiberius's brother-in-law, the current CEO of Stone Properties? That explains why Tiberius had collected information on George Barnes. But what does it mean?"

"The article says Preston was traveling cross-country on his way to attend college on the East Coast. Thought he'd go out and do a little hiking."

Despite the weird sensation crawling up her spine, Scarlett couldn't discern anything in either the article or the photo that had prompted Grady's call. "I'm not sure I understand what's so important about this information."

"Look more closely at George Barnes." Grady was buzzing with excitement. "Does he remind you of anyone?"

"No. Yes. I'm not really sure."

"He looks like JT Stone."

"What?" Scarlett looked closer and the pieces slipped into place. "You're right. What are you thinking, that this George Barnes guy and the Stone family are related somehow?"

"No." Grady grew serious. "I'm thinking that Barnes and Preston Rhodes are the same guy."

"How is that possible?" Then a door in her mind opened and a hundred detective-show plots raced through her brain. "You think George Barnes stole Preston Rhodes's identity?"

"Why not? Barnes's file paints a picture of a kid with no future. Mom's a hooker. Dad's probably one of her clients. He'd been in and out of the foster care system. Spent some time in juvy. Three of his buddies in the photo are in prison. Then he meets Preston Rhodes, a kid his own age who has money and no family, and who's moving clear across the country to go to college. Who would know if George Barnes put his wallet in the dead kid's pocket and assumed Preston's identity?"

"And when Tiberius found out…" Scarlett stopped breathing as she absorbed the implication. "You think that's why he was killed."

"Makes a good motive."

It certainly did. Perhaps it was time to let the police know what they'd discovered.

As Logan was turning into his driveway, his cell rang. It was Scarlett.

"Logan, you won't believe what Grady and I found in

Tiberius's files." She sounded both exhilarated and anxious. "We might have figured out who killed him."

Logan entered his house and made a beeline for Madison's room. Earlier that afternoon his sister had called. Madison hadn't done as he'd asked and called her parents. Nor was she answering her phone. Giving her the summer to change her mind about college wasn't working. It was time for her to go home.

"The police already have a suspect in custody. A detective buddy of mine has been keeping me updated on the case and he called to tell me that a little after noon today."

Madison's bedroom had an empty, unlived-in feel. No clothes cluttered the chair by the window. The dresser wasn't littered with jewelry and cosmetics. Even as he crossed to the closet, his instinct told him what he'd find. Nothing. His niece was gone.

"Are they sure they have the right guy?" Scarlett's doubt came through loud and clear.

"Positive." Cursing, he retraced his steps down the hall and found a folded piece of paper on the breakfast bar. "He confessed that he was hired by Councilman Scott Worth to silence Tiberius and get a hold of some documents that proved he was embezzling campaign contributions."

"That's what he stole from my suite?"

"And grabbed some other random files to hide his true purpose."

Madison had taken off for L.A. again. No wonder she wasn't answering her cell. What the hell was she thinking?

"Oh, well, good." Scarlett sounded less enthusiastic than she should.

"Did you ever talk to Madison?" he asked.

"No. I was going to and then Grady called." Scarlett sounded subdued. "Have you tried her cell?"

"She's not answering. She took off for L.A."

"No," Scarlett assured him. "She wouldn't do that. Not without talking to me first."

"Well, she did."

"Damn." Worry vibrated through Scarlett's tone. "I really thought I'd gotten through to her."

"I think you did," Logan said. "Only not about college. Ever since that producer friend of yours came into town, Madison has had nothing but stars in her eyes. And you didn't do anything to dissuade her." Even as he took his frustration out on her, Logan recognized it was unfair to blame Scarlett when he had a truckload of regrets at how he'd handled Madison yesterday. "Can you try her cell? Her mother and I aren't having any luck getting her to pick up. Maybe she'll answer for you."

"Sure." Her voice was neutral and polite. "And then I'll call Bobby to see if he's heard from her."

"Is he trustworthy?"

"Absolutely. She won't get into trouble with him."

"What about the rest of the people she's bound to meet?" His concern came out sounding like accusation.

Scarlett's answer was slower in coming. "She's a smart girl, Logan. She'll be careful."

"She's ambitious and overly optimistic."

"I told her in no uncertain terms how hard the business is," Scarlett countered. "She isn't as naive as you think."

"She's only eighteen."

"I get that you're worried about her, Logan."

"Do you? She was hoping to stay with you in L.A." He knew Madison had enough money from her birthday and from what she'd earned working for Scarlett to put herself up in a decent hotel for a week or so. Longer if she chose something on the seedier side. "Where is she going to go if you aren't there?"

"This isn't her first trip to L.A. I know she has friends

there she kept in touch with. She'll probably crash with one of them. Let me try calling her. I'll let you know in a couple minutes if I get ahold of her."

While he waited for Scarlett to call back, Logan stared out the sliding glass door at the pool where Madison loved to hang out. The sun sparkling off the water was blinding, but he stared at the turquoise rectangle until his eyes burned. Although part of him agreed with Scarlett that Madison was capable of taking care of herself, the other part recognized that he'd been tasked with a job and had failed miserably at it. Paula was going to kill him when she found out he'd lost her baby.

His cell rang after what seemed like forever, but the clock on the microwave revealed it had only been ten minutes.

"Her phone must be off. It's rolling straight to voice mail," Scarlett said. "So I called Bobby. He hasn't heard from her, but he promised to call me as soon as he does."

"Thanks." He sounded grim.

"She was determined to go to L.A., Logan. We all may have been kidding ourselves that she intended to go to college this fall. When there's something Madison wants, she goes after it. You should all be proud of her. I wish I'd had half her confidence at her age."

"You expect me to be proud?" he demanded, his voice an impatient whip. "She ran off without letting anyone know her plans."

"Maybe it was the only way she could do what she wanted."

Logan didn't want to hear what Scarlett was trying to tell him. "What happens when this acting thing doesn't pan out?"

"She can always go to college."

"Like you did?"

An uncomfortable silence filled the phone's speaker before Scarlett replied. "Madison and I grew up very differently. I started acting when I was nine. That's all I knew. I didn't have the opportunity to choose what I wanted to do at eighteen. By then I'd been a star with all that came with it and was on my way to becoming a has-been. Maybe if I'd grown up around normal kids, gone to school, and the only expectations put on me were to go to college and get a regular job, I might have ended up a savvy businesswoman like Violet or Harper." Her voice took on a husky throb. "Or maybe I'd have ended up just like Madison, feeling trapped by what everyone else wanted me to be."

"You think Madison felt trapped by her parents' expectations?"

"And yours. You are a hard man to please, Logan."

"Is that what you've been trying to do?" he questioned, infuriated by her reproach. "Please me? Because if that's the case, you haven't been doing a very good job."

"It figures you'd see it that way. For a few days I thought our differences were behind us, but now I see they'll never be." She sounded immeasurably sad. "I knew this thing between us would be short, but it was way more fun than I could have hoped."

Logan's anger vanished at her declaration. He'd never imagined this phone call would lead here. "Scarlett—" Was she really ready to call it quits? Was he? "This is not the conversation we should be having right now."

"Why not? No reason to draw things out when it's so obvious that you blame me for Madison heading to L.A. I realize now that I'm always going to be doing something you disapprove of. And I need someone who has faith in me." She was trying to sound calm, but he could hear the emotion in her tone.

She stopped speaking and offered him a chance to respond. The violent rush of blood through his veins made his ears ring. She was giving him an opportunity to take back his accusations and abandon his disapproval of her past. Her silence pulled at him, but he couldn't form the words she wanted to hear.

"I have to go," Scarlett said. "I've got something important waiting for me. I'll call you if I hear from Bobby or Madison. Goodbye, Logan."

And then she was gone, leaving him to curse that he'd treated her badly when all she wanted to do was help. And thanks to his stubbornness, he'd lost her.

Overwhelmed by a whole new set of worries, Logan sat down at his kitchen table and tried to push his conversation with Scarlett out of his mind. First things first. He had to find Madison before she got into trouble.

Once that was accomplished, he could figure out what to do about Scarlett.

Unsure how she'd gone from walking on clouds this morning to trudging through mud this evening, Scarlett turned back to the photos Grady had uncovered. She'd sent the man home to shower, eat and sleep an hour ago. He hadn't gone without protest. Grady's passion for Las Vegas history was boundless. It's why she'd hired him to develop her Mob Experience exhibit. Days of sifting through Tiberius's files had yielded many things of interest, but little that Grady didn't already know. This recent discovery was something completely new and not wholly related to Las Vegas.

She should drop it. Preston Rhodes was not the sort of man you accused of criminal activities without a whole lot of solid evidence. And she had none.

Scarlett slipped everything into the folder marked George Barnes. A business card had been stapled to the manila file. It belonged to an L.A. reporter by the name of Charity Rimes. On a whim, Scarlett pocketed the card. Just because Tiberius's killer had been caught didn't mean she had to drop the mystery of Preston Rhodes and George Barnes.

After that, Scarlett left the storage room. Her fight with Logan moved to the forefront of her mind as she walked to her car. What was she thinking to push him away like she had? Sure, he'd taken his frustration out on her, but it wasn't the first time. Now, thanks to her impulsiveness, it would probably be the last. What had she done?

But she couldn't just blame herself. It stung that he continued to throw her lack of a formal education in her face. Granted, a business degree would have helped her when she'd first taken over Fontaine Richesse, but she'd always been a quick study and had mastered her responsibilities faster than anyone expected.

Why couldn't he appreciate that she was better at thinking outside the box than either of her sisters? Street smarts had to count for something. She understood how people's greedy nature could get the best of them and made sure her marketing appealed to their desire for fun and profit. Granted, she might not pull in Violet's younger sophisticated crowd or Harper's überwealthy clientele, but her casino was always packed and always bringing in huge profits.

On her way back to the hotel, she worried over the fact that she had too few answers and too many questions. Madison. Logan. Tiberius's files. Her thoughts spun like a hamster on a wheel, going faster and faster but getting nowhere.

Instead of heading straight for Fontaine Richesse, she drove to Violet's hotel for a liberal dose of her sister's optimism.

She found Violet in the middle of Fontaine Chic's casino,

with her long dark hair pulled back into a smooth ponytail. Violet's evening style was like her hotel, elegant, sleek and cosmopolitan. Dark eye shadow made her eyes pop in her pale face. Crystal chandelier earrings swung from her earlobes. Her form-hugging black dress showed off her lean lines and toned legs.

"Got a second?" Scarlett asked as she approached. "I need to talk to you. I really blew it with Logan and I don't know how to fix it."

"Come with me while I check on things at Baccarat." She was referring to the stylish lobby bar that overlooked the strip. "We can sit down and you can tell me what happened."

Scarlett settled in a quiet corner of the bar while Violet went to speak with her bartender. He seemed more animated than usual and their conversation stretched out for longer than Scarlett expected. While she waited for Violet's return, her gaze drifted over the crowd. As usual, the young and beautiful occupied the sofas and chairs. Violet's hotel attracted a twenty-something clientele from L.A., New York and Miami. They liked to party more than gamble, but when they did hit the casino, they spent more than a dozen of Scarlett's customers combined.

One man stood out from the other bar patrons. With a jolt, Scarlett recognized him. JT Stone, Tiberius's nephew. What was he doing here? Scarlett followed the direction of his gaze. Staring at Violet is what he was doing here.

"That's JT Stone," Scarlett said as Violet sat down on the sofa beside her. "I'm surprised he's here."

"He comes by most nights around this time."

"You know he's staring at you, right?"

"It's just his way of telling me he's angry because I stole Rick away." Violet nodded toward the bartender who was whipping up one of his legendary cocktails.

"He doesn't look angry. He looks hungry." Scarlett paused for effect. "For you."

Violet waved her hand dismissively. "Why don't you tell me what happened with you and Logan."

Despite Baccarat's dim lighting, Scarlett spied bright color in Violet's cheeks. But rather than torment her sister with more questions, Scarlett decided to let the matter drop. For now.

"Madison took off for L.A. and Logan blames me." Scarlett paused as the waitress brought their drinks. Eager to see what Rick had made for them, she took a sip. It was a spicy blend of jalapeño and lime with just a hint of sweetness. "Delicious."

Violet coughed, probably caught off guard by the punch of heat. "I'm not sure this is one of my favorites."

"It's definitely not for everyone." Scarlett tasted the cocktail again.

"You two have fought before," Violet reminded her.

"Not like this. He said things. I said things." Scarlett felt hot tears fill her eyes. "I think I told him that I was done."

"You think you told him?"

"I didn't actually come right out and say that I never wanted to speak to him again."

"What did you say exactly?"

"I think I told him I need someone who has faith in me." She'd been so hurt that words had just poured out of her. "He makes me feel as if everything I do is wrong."

"You two have very different ways of approaching things." Violet patted her hand. "What did he say?"

"Nothing. I gave him a chance to tell me that he believed in me, or to tell me that not everything I do is wrong, but he didn't say anything. So I ended the call."

"It doesn't sound like you two are done."

"It sure feels that way. I can't imagine a future with a man who can't love me, faults and all."

"Give him a little time to calm down. From everything you've said, being in charge of Madison has been really stressful for him. I'm sure he simply overreacted to her going to L.A. without warning."

Scarlet wanted very much for Violet to be right, but wasn't sure she could make herself believe that she was.

"Thanks for listening to me," Scarlett said, forcing herself to smile past the ache in her throat. "Now let me give you a piece of advice. Take JT one of these." Scarlett lifted her glass and smirked at her sister over the rim. "Unless, of course, you think he's already hot enough."

Violet scowled at her, but the burst of color was back in her cheeks. With a laugh, Scarlett finished her cocktail and bid her sister goodbye.

On her way back to Fontaine Richesse, Scarlett's fingers itched to dial Logan's number. She was desperate to find out if he'd heard from Madison, but decided to heed Violet's advice to give him some space.

Scarlett returned to her office. Normally she would go down and make sure everything was running smoothly in the casino, but tonight she needed some uninterrupted time to sort through the day's revelations.

The message light on her office phone made her heart leap. Maybe Madison had returned her call. But it was Logan who had left the message. He was heading to L.A. to find his niece. Why hadn't he called her cell? The most obvious answer was he hadn't wanted to talk to her.

She dropped into her desk chair with a frustrated exhale, her thoughts coming full circle. Maybe she'd been right to end things. Logan showed no sign that he'd stop treating her like a friendly enemy and start regarding her as his partner. On the other hand, the chemistry between them was explosive enough to make it worth their while to find some middle ground.

Of course, Logan's steely determination wasn't conducive to compromising any more than her stubborn streak made her easy to get along with. But she'd sacrificed a fabulous part in a television series in order to stay in Las Vegas and be with Logan. And he'd tracked her down at her suite to ask that she not leave town. Surely that spoke to change for both of them.

Scarlett couldn't stop thinking that if she'd called Madison today the teenager might not have headed to L.A. Nor was she happy with the idea of sitting around and waiting for the situation to resolve itself. What she needed to do was head to L.A. and track Madison down. She'd convince the eighteen-year-old to give up acting and choose college. Logan would then see that she might make mistakes, but she could fix them, as well.

Decision made, Scarlett booked a plane ticket for the next morning and called Sandy to let her know she was going to L.A. Next, she called her second in command and put him in charge of the hotel with instructions to contact her if anything serious arose. She doubted he'd have any problems. The hotel had been running smoothly for months with only the occasional blip.

In a cab on the way to the airport, Scarlett debated calling Logan and letting him know she was coming. In the end, she decided not to give him the opportunity to say no to her help. On the other hand, he wasn't a man who appreciated being surprised. If she found Madison and he didn't know she was in L.A. looking, he would be angry. Her earlier reflection on their relationship determined her course of action. If she wanted Logan to consider her a partner, she needed to be open and up-front with him. Even if it went against her normal operating procedure to do so.

Not surprisingly, her call ended up in voice mail. Once she'd delivered the news that she was on her way to join him, she sat back and waited for the explosion. But when her phone rang it was Chase.

"Madison decided to take off and go to L.A.," she explained. "I'm on my way there now. I hoped maybe you'd heard from her."

"And here I was thinking you wanted to get together and relive old times."

Scarlett forced her voice to relax. "I'm sure you have better things to do than that. Has Madison called you?"

"I gave her my number, but haven't heard from her."

"If she does call, would you let me know? We're all worried about her."

"Sure enough. And give me a call later if you want to get a drink."

"Thanks for the offer, but I've got my hands full at the moment."

"That Wolfe guy?"

"As a matter of fact, yes."

"I figured the way he was mooning over you and glaring at me." He sounded amused. "If he doesn't treat you like you deserve, let me know. I'll kick his ass."

Scarlett grinned. "Thanks, Chase. You're a pal." She hung up just as the flight attendant announced that all electronic devices needed to be shut off and stowed. Logan hadn't called. Anxiety stretched her nerves thin. It was going to be an agonizing hour or so until the plane landed in L.A.

# Eleven

As he sat behind the wheel of his rental car glaring at the traffic clogging the 110 Freeway, Logan decided that coming to L.A. had been an impulsive, rash idea. Nothing that he'd accomplished today couldn't have been done from the comfort of his air-conditioned office at Wolfe Security. Randolph had put him in touch with the private investigator they'd used the last time they'd tracked Madison down and he'd met with the guy an hour after touching down in L.A.

Now, he was heading back to LAX. Not to return to Las Vegas, but to meet Scarlett's flight. When he'd left her a message last night, he'd half expected, half hoped she'd jump on a plane and come to L.A. He was damned glad she was on her way.

It was hard on a stubborn bachelor like him to realize that Scarlett's absence hit him physically as well as psychologically. He had an ache in his gut that hadn't subsided since she'd hung up on him yesterday afternoon. She'd only been trying to help and he'd criticized the choices she'd made in her youth. The same choices that had created the strong, sexy, sometimes vulnerable woman who gave herself to him completely in bed and kept him guessing the rest of the time.

In the past twelve hours he'd come to the realization that what had bloomed between them wasn't just sexual. His heart ached with emotions too strong to contain and too new to voice. But he had to try.

Standing near the gate exit, Logan couldn't ignore the churning in his stomach. He was anxious to see her. Eager to apologize for taking his frustration with Madison out on her.

And then she was sauntering in his direction. Accustomed to her vibrant energy, he wasn't prepared for how pale and subdued she looked and hated the worry lines etched between her eyebrows. His heart thundered against his ribs as she spotted him waiting for her. Before his lips formed a hello, she held up her hand to forestall whatever he'd been about to say.

"Don't be mad at me for coming," she said. "I'm just as worried about Madison as you are and I know it's my fault she's here."

"I was wrong to blame you. Madison is strong-willed and once she sets her mind to something, there's no swaying her." The need to find his niece weighed on him, but so did the damage he'd done to his relationship with Scarlett. "About our last conversation…"

She shook her head, but wouldn't meet his gaze. "Not until we find Madison." When he began to protest, she cut him off. "Promise me. We need to keep the focus on her."

"Fine," he told her, cupping her face and staring into her beautiful eyes. "But I'm not happy about it."

"I didn't expect you to be." The throb in her voice gave

away more than her expression. She was wary of him in a way she'd never been before.

The end to their last conversation sprang to mind and his joy in her arrival dimmed. Why did he feel as if she was only here to tie up the loose ends of their relationship so she could have a clean break with him?

Logan relieved her of the overnight bag she carried and took her free hand, gratified that she didn't try to pull away. "The car's parked this way."

"Have you had any luck locating Madison?"

"No. I've called the boy she followed out here last spring and made contact with the private detective my brother-in-law hired once before, but no luck."

"You should never have let me near her," Scarlett said. "If she'd worked with either Violet or Harper she never would've met Bobby and been encouraged to pursue acting."

"Maybe." Logan drew her into the warm Los Angeles evening. "Or maybe she was playing all of us this summer and never intended to go to college in the fall."

"But she said…" Scarlett trailed off and frowned. "If you're right, she's a better actress than I ever was."

"I know that's not true."

Scarlett laughed. "You've never seen me act."

"I've seen everything you've ever done."

"That's impossible."

He felt the weight of her disbelief as he unlocked the doors on his rental car and ushered her inside. Before he closed the door, he took ahold of her gaze. "What can I say? I'm a fan."

Shutting the door on her stunned expression offered him a moment of amusement. She had shifted sideways on the seat and was poised to get answers as soon as he slid behind the wheel.

"Since when?" she demanded as he started the car.

"I think I saw you for the first time when you starred on *That's Our Hilary*."

"Don't tell me you watched that."

"Not me. My sister, Paula. Her, Lucas and I used to fight over who got to watch what. We outnumbered her, but she was older by a year and always got first choice. I really learned to hate that show." He flashed her a wicked grin. "Lucas thought you were hot."

Her eyes narrowed. "I thought you said you were a fan."

"You were really amazing in *Sometimes Forever*."

"Do you really expect me to believe that you watched that show? It really isn't your thing." Her self-assurance began to slip a little, exposing her quieter, fragile core. "And there weren't more than eight episodes. It never even made it to DVD."

"When you first came to Las Vegas, as much as we rubbed each other the wrong way, I couldn't stop thinking about you. I found and watched everything you'd done because I had you pegged as just some woman who read lines someone else had written." He took her hand in his and lifted her fingers to his lips. "It really bugged me that not only were you beautiful and fascinating in whatever role you played, you also brought great depth to your characters."

"But ever since I've known you, you've been nothing but critical of my career." Her green eyes went soft with confused hurt. "Why, when you felt like that?"

Admitting that he was wrong was like swallowing foul-tasting medicine. He knew it was good for him, but hated the punishment on his senses. "Because I might be able to step outside the box and see all the possibilities in a computer program or security system, but when it comes to people, I take a narrow view."

She cocked her head. "Is that your way of telling me you're sorry for being such a judgmental ass?"

"Sorry?" He winced dramatically and watched her outrage grow. "I'm not sure I'd go that far." When her lips popped open to chastise him, he cupped her cheek in his palm and leaned closer so she couldn't miss the sincerity in his gaze. "You make me want to be a better man."

"I think you're pretty terrific already."

"You must be in love with me," he declared, kissing her on the nose.

"Why would you say that?" She tried for a light tone, but it came out sounding a little too anxious.

"Because only a woman in love would think I'm terrific after I took my anxiety and exasperation out on her earlier."

"Oh, that." She waved her hand in dismissal. "I'm just used to your bad-tempered ways."

She took his hand. The feel of her fingers meshed with his lowered his blood pressure and calmed the agitation he'd been feeling since she'd hung up on him yesterday.

She, too, looked more at ease as they exited the parking ramp. Silence reigned as he got them onto the freeway and heading north.

"I'm all out of ideas where we should look for Madison next," he said, prodding her out of her thoughts.

"I called Chase before the plane left Las Vegas, but he hadn't heard from her."

"I can't believe she'd call him."

"Why not?" Scarlett smiled. "Chase might be a mega star, but he's also a great guy. He's never forgotten the help he had on the way up and donates a ton of his time to charities. He likes to give back. And he really hit it off with Madison."

"He seems to hit it off with you, as well." Logan made no attempt to conceal his irritation.

"We've worked together."

"It seemed more familiar than I would expect between two colleagues."

"We might have dated briefly."

That piece of information didn't surprise Logan, but it made his heart feel like a cumbersome weight in his chest. "Was it serious?"

Scarlett stared out the side window. "We were young." Her phone began to ring before Logan could press further. "It's Madison."

Logan saw his niece's smiling face on Scarlett's phone screen. Relief rushed through him.

Scarlett keyed the speaker. "Madison, oh, thank heavens. I left you three messages. Are you all right?"

"Fine. I forgot my charger when I packed for L.A. and my phone died. I finally got around to buying a new one."

"Well, I'm glad you did. Logan's here with me. We've been frantic. Why didn't you tell us you were headed to L.A.?"

"I left a note for Logan."

"I wish you'd talked with me instead," Logan said.

"You don't talk," Madison complained. "You command."

"I can't argue with you there." Scarlett spared Logan a brief glance and saw his lips tighten. "But didn't you think you could tell me what was going on?"

"I should have, but I was so mad at Uncle Logan and you two are so tight these days...."

But not so tight anymore. The thought tempered her joy in finding out Madison was okay.

"Besides, I wanted to surprise you once everything was finalized," the teenager continued.

"Once what was finalized?" Logan asked.

"I'm going to attend UCLA in the fall."

"UCLA?" Scarlett silently demanded answers from

Logan, but he shook his head. "That's wonderful. How come you didn't mention that you'd been accepted there?"

"Because I didn't know. I never got an acceptance letter and assumed that they'd rejected me."

"But they didn't?"

"No. Turns out my parents intercepted the letter and didn't tell me I'd gotten in. It was my top choice because it's in L.A. and they've got a fantastic school of theater, film and television. I was devastated when the letters went out last March and I didn't get one."

Is that what had accounted for her running off to L.A. last spring? Scarlet exchanged a glance with Logan. "So how did you find out you were accepted?"

"They also posted the acceptances online. I was so bummed about the letter, I completely forgot that I could find out from their website until I was clearing out old emails yesterday and found the ID and password."

"I'm thrilled for you," Scarlett said, giddy with relief and delight. "So you came to L.A. to…?"

"Tour the campus and check out the dorms."

"Of course." Weak with relief, she grinned at Logan. "Where are you? We'll come pick you up and take you out for a celebratory dinner."

"You're in L.A.?"

"Logan and I came here looking for you."

"You really were worried." Madison sounded as if she finally realized the impact of what she'd done. "I'm sorry, but I can't do dinner. I already have plans with some of the people I met last time I was out here."

"Where are you staying?"

"With them. They're going to drop me off at the terminal after breakfast tomorrow so I can catch the bus back to Las Vegas."

"We could come get you. Fly you back to Las Vegas with us."

"Why don't you and Logan hang out in L.A. for a few days? I'll be fine."

And Scarlett knew she would be. "We'll catch up tomorrow and let you know our plans. Have fun." She didn't bother to add "be safe."

After disconnecting the call, Scarlett said, "I'm guessing her parents are not going to be happy she got into UCLA."

"To hell with them," Logan growled. "They're getting what they want. She's going to college. The least they can do is let her attend the school of her choice."

Nothing could have demonstrated what a tough month it had been for Logan better than those words. Scarlett kissed her fingertips and pressed them against his cheek.

"You're going to make a fabulous father someday," she declared, grinning broadly. "As much as you grumble and complain about her, you've been behind her all along. She might not tell you so, but I know she appreciates that you haven't dictated to her like her parents did and that you were willing to support her choice of whatever college she went to. She's lucky to have you."

"Thanks." Logan captured her hand and pressed a sizzling kiss into her palm. "Now that we've accomplished our mission, where should go to celebrate?"

"Why don't we head up to Malibu? I have a house on the beach."

"You keep a house here?"

"It was the first thing I bought when I turned eighteen. I know it doesn't make sense to keep a three-million-dollar piece of property sitting around empty, but I love it too much to sell."

If he'd found out about this a week ago he would have been utterly convinced that Scarlett perceived her stay in

Vegas as a temporary one, but he was coming to accept that L.A. would always be a part of who she was.

"I can understand that. I have a place in Aspen that I don't get to often enough anymore, but I can't bear the thought of giving up the skiing."

"Oh, hot tubbing after a day on the slopes. Sounds heavenly."

"We'll have to go there this winter."

"I'd like that," she began, her voice sounding peculiar. "But…"

He shot her a glance and was surprised at how concerned she looked. "Time to talk?"

She directed him onto Interstate 10 before answering, "Let's wait until we get to my house."

Little more passed between them until they reached the Pacific Coast Highway. Scarlett could tell Logan had a lot on his mind, but for once she wasn't interested in knowing what it was. As they drew closer to her house, she warned him so he wouldn't miss her driveway.

"I hope you like it," she said, unlocking the front door and leading the way into a spacious white living room with tiled floors, a turquoise-blue couch and panoramic views of the Pacific. "I called ahead and had the property management company stock the fridge. I thought we could have dinner and take a walk on the beach."

"That sounds nice," he said, regarding her intently. "Where do you want me to put the bags?"

The question hung in the air between them.

"It would be easy to tell you the master bedroom," she responded. "So many things are wrong between us, but sexual chemistry isn't one of them."

Scarlett threw open the sliding glass doors that opened onto the oceanside terrace and let in the breeze.

"Yesterday you said you needed someone who had faith in you," Logan said, coming up behind her.

Even though he didn't touch her, Scarlett felt his presence like a caress, and it was hard not to lean back against him. "And I gave you ample opportunity to say you did."

Logan put his hand on her upper arm and spun her to face him. "I've given you no reason to grant me another chance, but I wish you would."

Scarlett couldn't believe what she was hearing. "I don't know why you're asking. No matter how hard I try not to irritate you, I'm eventually going to do something and you're going to get mad."

"Would you believe me if I told you that I like being upset by you?"

"No." But her eyes sparkled with amusement.

"How about if I told you that you've made me happier than I've ever been?"

She grew somber. "Then I consider my work here finished."

"You can't mean that."

"I don't, but the way things are between us, I can't see our future being anything but one long argument."

"If this is about your accusation that I don't believe in you, that's not true."

Logan's scowl made hope flare in Scarlett's heart, but could she trust his declaration?

"I'm only speaking from what you've said and how you've behaved."

"Including the night I showed up at your place demanding you stay in Las Vegas?"

"Yes." She would forever cherish the memory of that night. "And how, less than twenty-four hours later, you were furious at me. And that the day before you couldn't wait to find out when your life was going to get back to normal."

Logan looked chastened by her words, but he continued to argue. "That's when I thought you were leaving. I didn't want you to go, but couldn't bring myself to ask you to stay."

"So you pushed me away?"

"It's how I react when I'm feeling vulnerable. I did the same thing to Elle all those years ago. I wanted her to choose me, but I was too proud to ask her to. I was bullheaded and wrong, and I almost made the same mistake with you."

"But you were in love with Elle."

"I'm in love with you."

For a second Scarlett gaped at him. "No wa—"

Logan silenced the flow of her words with a kiss. Startled by the abruptness of his lips against her, she nevertheless surrendered to the flood of heat and emotion his touch inspired. Any thoughts of dinner or a walk on the beach fled. She was flushed and dizzy by the time he lifted his lips from hers.

"Marry me."

Fearing wishful thinking had made her mishear him, Scarlett didn't answer. Her heart was pounding so hard she thought her chest would explode.

"I'm sorry," she said at last. "I don't think I heard you correctly."

"I asked you to marry me."

"Now I'm certain I'm not hearing you correctly."

He scowled at her. "Stop turning this romantic moment into a comedy."

"Well, excuse me if I'm caught a little off guard." Despite her tone, she couldn't stop grinning. "Of course, I'll marry you."

"That's great," he told her, an edge of impatience to

his voice. "Because I love you and I don't think I can live without you."

"You don't think?" she prompted, nuzzling his neck and nipping at his earlobe. "Or you know you can't?"

"I'm pretty damned sure that I am going to be very happy spending the rest of my life being aggravated by you in the best and worst possible way."

"That's my guy," she murmured, kissing him with all the love in her heart and glorying in the love she got back. "I'm pretty smitten with you myself."

"Smitten enough to test for the project Bobby came down to talk to you about?"

She pulled back far enough to scrutinize his expression. "I thought you understood that I'd decided to pass."

"I understand that you love to act. And I understand that the part is perfect for you. What I don't understand is why you decided to pass when Bobby was willing to bend over backwards to accommodate your schedule."

How could she make him see what she couldn't quite grasp herself? "I'm afraid."

"Of what?"

Where did she start? "Not being good enough. That if I don't give my full attention to the hotel, something bad will happen." And in a smaller voice, "Losing you."

"You'll be wonderful. You have the best-run hotel on the Strip." He kissed her slow and deep. "As for losing me, that will never happen. You're the most amazing thing that's ever happened to me."

Her throat tightened almost painfully. His faith bolstered her courage. Snug in his arms, Scarlett dared to consider whether she could have the two things in the world she loved most.

"I suppose I could call Bobby in the morning and see if we could meet with him to talk about schedules." She framed Logan's face with her hands and peered deep into his eyes. "As long as you understand that you'll always be my first priority. I can live without acting. I can't live without you."

"That's the one thing you don't have to worry about," he promised, espresso eyes soft and warm as they toured her face. "I'm never going to let you go."

\* \* \* \* \*

*If you liked this story, try these other novels from Cat Schield:*

*MEDDLING WITH A MILLIONAIRE*
*A WIN-WIN PROPOSITION*
*UNFINISHED BUSINESS*
*A TRICKY PROPOSITION*
*THE NANNY TRAP*

*All available now from Harlequin Desire!*

# REQUEST YOUR FREE BOOKS!
## 2 FREE NOVELS PLUS 2 FREE GIFTS!

**(H) HARLEQUIN®**

*Desire*

ALWAYS POWERFUL, PASSIONATE AND PROVOCATIVE